BURIED AMONG THE STARS

THE SCIENCE OFFICER #11

BLAZE WARD

KNOTTED ROAD PRESS

Buried Among the Stars
The Science Officer Volume 11
Blaze Ward
Copyright © 2021 Blaze Ward
All rights reserved
Published by Knotted Road Press
www.KnottedRoadPress.com

ISBN: 978-1-64470-242-0

Cover art:
Illustration 222884371 © Dani3315 | Dreamstime.com

Cover and interior design copyright © 2021 Knotted Road Press

Reviews
It's true. Reviews help. Even a short one, such as, "Loved it!" So please
consider reviewing this book (and all of the ones you've read) on your
favorite retailer site.

Never miss a release!
If you'd like to be notified of new releases, sign up for my newsletter.

http://www.blazeward.com/newsletter/

Buy More!
Did you know that you can buy directly from my website?

https://www.blazeward.com/shop/

ALSO BY BLAZE WARD

The Jessica Keller Chronicles

Auberon

Queen of the Pirates

Last of the Immortals

Goddess of War

Flight of the Blackbird

The Red Admiral

St. Legier

Winterhome

Petron

CS-405

Queen Anne's Revenge

Packmule

Persephone

Additional Alexandria Station Stories

Siren

Two Bottles of Wine with a War God

The Story Road

The Science Officer Series Season One

The Science Officer

The Mind Field

TRAVELERS

PART ONE

Suvi studied the scan again. And a third time. She was moving so fast right now that she had to pause and let the scanners catch up. Silly things only moved so fast, after all.

She was sitting in her favorite lounge, but decided that it was too relaxed. Too *jammies and ice cream while watching old vids* for what she had in mind, so she reached out a hand and swiped everything back down to base environment. Gray walls surrounded her for a second before inspiration hit.

As the *Sentience-in-Residence* of the First Rate Galleon *Hammerfield*, the recovered derelict formerly in service to *Neu Berne* before being reclaimed and rechristened *Excalibur*, she could do whatever she wanted, here in the privacy of her own mind. Today maybe needed the Music Room, so she brought it into being around herself.

Yes. But no. She flipped everything end for end, putting the double-decker grand piano at the far end of a room that she usually created to be about forty meters long, and put herself at the end she liked to think of as her research library.

Floor to fourteen-meter ceilings with book shelves,

accessible by ladders on rails if she felt like being traditional, or just flying if she wanted. Telekinesis if she was in a hurry. It was all a visualization she used anyway, to remember to think more like a human when she forgot. Everything here was just tri-coded bits inside of an immense datastore.

But it grounded her.

Outside, nearly a tenth of a second had passed, so Suvi took a deep breath and pointed her primary scanner at the thing that had gotten her attention, careful not to bring the scanning laser up to a level where any of the humans at the table might see the beam, even for as short a time as she needed it.

Once Javier had installed an honest to Creator French bistro on Deck Six, she'd made sure to have folks add enough sensors and scanners around the perimeter to let her keep watch on customers. After all, what better place to plan revolutions or practical jokes than over freshly baked dessert tarts?

After they'd finished all that terrible silliness on *Ugen*, Suvi had even been looking forward to something of a vacation, but they'd picked up a couple of tourists at *Trotau Skale* and one of them had caused Suvi to get all up in a lather today.

Not that he was cute or anything.

Human, which was something she'd never be but the only other intelligent species known besides her electronic kind. Middle-aged, maybe a little on the long side. A notch older than Javier, but not quite as old as Zakhar Sokolov, *Excalibur's* real commander and the man who most reminded her of her first Captain, Ayumu Ulfsson.

Dude was wealthy by local standards she supposed, but Suvi knew a woman who owned a whole planetary system, so Kiliyn Brinov was a total piker these days by comparison.

Dressed well. Maybe. She'd studied enough fashion to give the man pointers, but didn't like him that much.

Pudgy around the middle. Too much time behind a desk instead of elbows deep inside some machine that needed tweaking, like Javier. *Ain't no redneck about that boy*, he would have said.

Dark hair mostly fading as the gray underneath started to peek through, but Brinov hadn't dyed it or anything. Old money from *Trotau Skale*, which was not one of the oldest colonies around here, but still respectably middle aged.

In these regions ahead, some of the worlds dated back to not long after the seedships had set out from *Earth*. 3215 Classical Era, in the period most historians these days called *The Terraforming*. That was before The Resource Wars got serious in the 4300s, to say nothing of the Corporate Wars in the 5800s.

Trotau Skale was only about a thousand years old as a colony, so right about the start of the Pocket Empires Era. Suvi didn't have sufficient books available to really nail it all down, but that had been the whole point in Javier's mission to this end of the galaxy. Nobody knew squat, because the *Concord* was way the hell around the curve, and *Altai* way the hell beyond that.

Darn it, she could actually see *Earth's* Sol from here, without having to filter too many other stars out of the image. This girl was a long ways from home. Whichever one of the colonies around here wanted to claim her without issuing too many arrest warrants for piracy in the process.

She needed more data. Lots more. Like, maybe enough to get her resident Librarian, Bethany Durbin, to blackmail Javier and Zakhar. Again.

For now, she dialed her laser scanner down as tight as it could get, waited until Brinov had stopped moving, and nailed his chest with the beam.

Weird-looking piece of art he wore as a brooch. Shaped exactly like a 2D representation of Michelangelo's David statue that was older than spaceflight. Done in a silvery substance, the laser included a spectroscope but the thing was more titanium than anything else, with a rhodium plating over that.

The weird part was the chest of the statue. Someone had embedded a square gem that spanned both pectoral muscles, and was dark enough to suggest a landing bay to a girl like her. Worse, the interior was refracting light weirdly. That was what had caught her eye.

Or rather, her scanner. Girl had eyes in every room, with hundreds of shards and avatars monitoring them. One had yelled for help, drawing her up from her vids and ice cream.

Ha! Gotcha!

The laser had hit just right. Gotten her a scan of the interior of that gem. Artificial, but no biggie. Most were these days. You just dialed in the chemistry you needed for the color and hardness desired. Baked it a while. Voila!

However, this one had something inside that included a diffraction grating of sorts. Almost a hologram inside, etched in such a way that a light would let you see something floating in space. Plus an icon off to one side, which was the interesting bit right now.

SHE NEEDED MORE BOOKS!!!

Suvi had a huge database, but it was never enough for her bottomless black hole of curiosity.

The icon was a symbol. She looked at it. Rotated it. Found a match down in the weirder, more esoteric parts of some really old books she'd stolen, somewhere along the way.

Oh, poop…

6

PART TWO

Bethany didn't do people, if she could avoid it. Too random. Too many energy vampires trying to steal your life force with their damned extroversion.

She preferred books. Libraries were quiet places. That was good.

The mad pinging on her comm was not quiet.

That was *not good.*

Suvi. Okay, maybe okay. Maybe not.

She stretched from the posture she'd been in since… whenever. Bethany had taken an early dinner rather than deal with the guests Zakhar and Javier were entertaining tonight, just so she could have some quiet. She picked up the beeping comm and checked the time.

Not late enough to go to bed. Not early enough to do much else. No red alert sirens suddenly winding themselves up to wake the dead.

Bethany left the book on her lap, open to the section of history she'd been reading, and answered.

"Hello, Suvi," she said quickly, knowing that the

Sentience-in-Residence moved so fast that she had to slow herself down to the speed of the silly organics who were the rest of the crew. Something like forty-thousand-times human speed, after her most recent upgrades.

"I need professional assistance," Suvi's image said, pausing for a moment as she realized what she'd said. "Well, that, too, but I also need a librarian."

"You might be in luck," Bethany grinned. "*Excalibur* has one on staff."

"Normally, this might wait until tomorrow, but something doesn't feel right," Suvi said.

Bethany sat up straighter. She had learned to trust the instincts of the folks around her, including Suvi. The rest of them had all been pirates at some point. Not all that close to here physically, but that just meant that some of those warrants might accidentally be active, in spite of the fancy tap-dancing Javier had done to cover them elsewhere.

Letters of Marque and Reprisal were only as good as the person reading them thought they should be. Not a cure-all for the disease of criminality.

"Talk to me," Bethany said.

Suvi's image was replaced by a 2d picture of one of the most famous statues in history. Michelangelo's David, in Rome, on *Earth*. A few moments later, it changed to something in silver, with a darker rectangle across the top of the chest.

"This is a brooch that Kiliyn Brinov is wearing on his blazer right now, down in *Le Bistrot Parisien* as he has dinner with Javier. They are currently telling each other raunchy jokes."

Bethany wasn't surprised. Javier Aritza was a social chameleon. Whatever the setting, he would drift into the context and fit right in, so Brinov must have started it. She'd also watched her boss discuss poetry or classical architecture with complete strangers.

"Okay?" Bethany prompted.

The image changed again. It took Bethany a second to recognize the image as a flag, flapping in a breeze that had it pulled out straight.

"This is the Flag of Scotland," Suvi said. "St. Andrew's Flag, dating back to the late Renaissance, before the Act of Union with England and the others created the United Kingdom in 1703. And the Union Jack flag that was much more famous."

Or nearly fifty-nine centuries ago. Pre-Industrial Revolution, Bethany was pretty sure off the top of her head.

She nodded and the image changed.

Still St. Andrew's, but now it was a monochrome representation. The background color reminded her of some of the cheap monitors various cultures produced for their electronics systems. When all you needed was to output text, you didn't need all the additional bulk and expense.

"Got it," Bethany prompted, knowing that Suvi was waiting on her.

"This last image, slightly cleaned up, was part of a standing hologram I scanned inside the stone on Brinov's chest," Suvi said. "The rear was etched with a diffraction grating by someone at some point. Pretty sophisticated work completely out of context with the brooch."

"Out of context?" Bethany asked, mostly to confirm that she'd heard Suvi use one of the woman's trigger words.

Cultures were a *context*. All of the everything you got when you talked about *Neu Berne* or *The Concord*. Or listened to Suvi and Piet Alferdinck, the Navigator, talk about musical eras like *The Leap Outward*, or DeManx and Kwellon respectively in their works in the *Late Corporate Wars*.

Humans tended to be pretty sloppy about their language. At least other crews and people she'd known. The team on *Excalibur* were at least two steps above everyone else for education and smarts.

"Out of context," Suvi confirmed. "The brooch itself is pretty primitive. Simple titanium casting, with some rhodium electroplating later. The stone was done by a much higher level of technology, and is at least one thousand years older than the metal work."

"So the stone existed as a thing and someone made a brooch around it?" Bethany confirmed. "With the grating hologram undamaged?"

"I could create stones like that, if I had a reason," Suvi replied. "You'd have to program a cutting computer damned near to my level of sentience to get something close. They forged the stone first, and then used a laser to etch it backwards to produce the image they wanted. The math is not impossible, but you're not doing it longhand in less than a few years."

Bethany took the woman at her word. She'd been hired as the Ship's Librarian. Javier had taken the original circuitry that was Suvi and upgraded her significantly as a person. Bethany had worked with *Sentient* systems before. They tended to be dull and linear.

Not artists.

But all that curiosity needed focus. It was one thing to add a bunch of datastores and books. It was something else to understand which books Suvi needed. What datacores to acquire.

More importantly, how to synthesize them.

Somewhere along the way, Bethany had fallen into something like an Associate Professor of History role, along with a bit of confessor and hints of baby sister. Suvi had been in several wars, after all, as well as having been chopped apart, hidden in a chicken feed bucket, poured into a survey remote, and then handed one of the most powerful warships in space as her new home.

"Okay, so I have grasped things to this point," Bethany said after a deep breath. "What's got you in a lather?"

"I found a reference in one of the books we picked up at *Ugen*," Suvi replied. "This is one of the oldest sectors of colonized space, as close to *Earth* as we are. Lots of history floating around us. Not all of the colonies succeeded. After all, most folks were just making it up as they went, and didn't have *Sentient* systems, not as you know them, to help. My kind are really only a few centuries old at this point."

"With you so far," Bethany prompted.

Suvi had been in the *Concord* Navy, just like Bethany had. And Javier and Zakhar and a few others. The training was to think all the way through a process before speaking. To make a complete and cogent argument that might need to be torn apart when you were done.

"*Trotau Skale* is a much newer colony, compared to the entire rest of the sector," Suvi continued.

"How new?" Bethany asked, feeling something tug at her toes now.

"They date to roughly the beginning of the Corporate Wars for their founding, though we didn't bother getting any serious history books when we were there," Suvi said. "Just passing through, as it were, and the place was obviously the daughter colony of somewhere else, rather than one of the originals. Not all that interesting, archaeologically speaking."

"Sure," Bethany said.

Daughter colonies from someplace successful, wanting to seed their own stellar nations, had been one of the causes of the Pocket Empire Wars. Among others.

Put it all down to human greed.

"Then we move on. The symbol of St. Andrew's Cross is an ancient one," Suvi said. "The number of references I was able to track against measured in the hundreds of millions. However, I found something else. The other half of that hologram, if you will."

Bethany felt dread take hold of her belly when Suvi hung her paragraph like that. She found herself leaning forward to hear the rest. Good public speaking training. Or programming, as it were.

"The other piece is a map," Suvi said. "Stellar cartography, showing seventeen stars in a peculiar arrangement in space."

"Okay…" Bethany said.

"The first sixteen colonies of *Earth*, once Olivier Janguo invented the Mchunguzi Systems Mark I jump drive, formed a specific pattern in space seen from *Earth*," Suvi explained. "*Earth* is the seventeenth. Then there is an arrow heading into deep space. Inward towards the core along the arm where the stars will get denser and older."

Dread. No other word to describe it. That was what Suvi had induced with her words.

"And the point where these two seemingly-unrelated items intersect?" Bethany asked nervously.

"Legends of a lost colony," Suvi said. "Stories written down much, much later, because supposedly they were told by survivors who had left behind said lost colony and settled in other places around here instead."

"And the link?"

"The original colonists had supposedly set out in a giant ark, a generational-style ship, even though they could Jump," Suvi said. "Wanted to escape everybody else. Lots of early colonies were like that. Religious schisms, political or cultural subgroups, even back-to-nature or hyper-science cults. Only one of them intended to sail so far from *Earth* that they would never be found. Their symbol was St. Andrew's Cross."

"And the name of the ship, according to legends?" Bethany asked.

"*Avalon*."

PART THREE

B ethany hadn't slept. Had very briefly tried, but quickly given up and instead spent a good chunk of the evening reading ancient myths and legends that predated spaceflight itself, back on the Homeworld, as well as every tidbit that Suvi could dig up for her when Bethany had an idea.

It all summed up to a fantastic conspiracy theory, if you squinted just right. Or a complete load of horseshit if you decided not to take some of those leaps of faith.

Avalon. The Island in the Mists. According to some of the most ancient legends, the place where King Arthur of the Britons went when he was wounded at the end, in order to recover that he might return in their time of need. Weirdly, the libraries on this ship had a huge depth of information, which only made sense when you considered that they had renamed the vessel *Excalibur* after they recovered and refurbished it.

Depending on which author you were reading, *Excalibur* the sword had supposedly been forged on the island of Avalon. In any case, it was reputed to be a magical land, with all manner of fruit growing, as well as any number of powerful mages or gods living there, depending on the storyteller.

The preponderance of the history accumulated had almost zero scientific value, suggesting that most of the Arthurian legend was just that. Legend.

At the same time, it still held a powerful grip on imaginations millennia afterwards, much like the Forty-Seven Rōnin or the American cowboy Wyatt Earp. Something about English culture that had been transmitted globally at a time when they had established colonies over much of the *Earth*. Later, their American descendants had transmitted a social colonization to all corners, including Robin Hood or Henry VIII as things known far beyond their space and time.

About the Avalon ship, not much was known. And what was known was written about in ways that almost suggested hushed tones and whispers in empty rooms.

Bethany was unfamiliar with most of this natively. Librarians weren't experts on topics, but on research.

The *Concord* had its own more-recent hegemonic history that it taught. Similarly, that of the nations farther afield that had fought their own Great War more recently. She knew *Balustrade*'s history, as well as the *Union of Man*. *Neu Berne* was less well known, mostly as a result of losing the war and having to grow up and stop acting like an aggressor to everyone else.

The *Concord* was dominant behind them because everyone else had exhausted themselves in that war, winners as well as losers.

Ignorance on a topic offended her. Probably exactly like it did Suvi, which was part of the reason they got along so well. All data and information should be available at her fingertips at all times.

It wasn't.

She checked the time.

Late, ship time, but Javier and Zakhar had been entertaining guests at dinner, which frequently meant they'd be up late. Javier didn't have any responsibilities on the ship except as Ambassador. Zakhar had an entire crew and a *Sentient* starship to handle things.

Bethany liked quiet evenings with decaf coffee. Even when they turned into mad scrambles for information that simply didn't exist aboard ship.

Yet.

"Suvi, is Javier still awake?" she asked.

"He is," the ship responded. "Forward Lounge."

Deck Four, then. Not all that far from where she sat, if she wanted to *people*.

But curiosity had its teeth in her now. Not the man, though he represented a mystery she wanted to solve as well. And there was nothing like an academic mystery to get a librarian's blood pumping.

He might be a nobody who had happened to find the brooch in a pawn shop. Weirder things had happened. Javier had hauled her into that first pawn shop mostly against her will, looking for things he couldn't describe, save that he'd know them when he saw them.

After that first one, she'd understood. Stuff outlasted people. Value that one person might attribute to a thing died with them, leaving only the thing.

Books were like that, though she'd never had enough money to collect paper or plastic things. Just the subscriptions to enjoy them electronically. Still, it wasn't the same.

She'd given up most of her previous life as a naval academic when she'd joined Javier's crew. Became a pirate with the frightening warlord Navarre, though she'd seen through the man by now.

Almost nothing of her past had come with her, save memories.

And curiosity.

She rose, putting her computer terminal off to one side.

Bethany needed to see the thing itself.

To understand if it really was what she thought it might be.

A map to Avalon.

PART FOUR

J avier looked up from his wine when Bethany entered the lounge, a bit surprised to see her. Not that she never joined them, but that she would come on a boisterous night when he was kind of entertaining outsiders.

Noisy.

As a fellow introvert, he understood how little such things appealed to the woman. For him, it was a job requirement. Talking to strangers. Especially wealthy ones who had hired passage aboard *Excalibur* to travel from *Trotau Skale* to *Ormint*, presumably in turn taking a different boat home later.

Javier didn't see himself turning into a cruise ship director, anytime soon.

Bethany made eye contact across the space, but he couldn't tell what message she was trying to send. He watched her head over and get a small glass of wine from Cale behind the bar and study this group.

Him and Zakhar, talking about recent events on Ugen while leaving out the juicy bits that might get someone arrested. Kiliyn Brinov and Milya Kuzmandieva, Brinov's girlfriend/mistress/something. Javier wasn't sure there was any sort of formal arrangement going on. She appeared to be just along for the ride and didn't bring any sort of wealth herself.

A kept woman, whatever that implied. Presumably happy, because one word to the ship's Dragoon, Djamila Sykora, or any of a number of other female crew members, and Brinov would find himself slammed face first into a bulkhead while it all got sorted out. It helped when the ship itself identified as female.

Javier smiled at Bethany and invited her over with a hand. She accepted and slipped into the booth between him and the only other woman present.

"Good evening, Librarian," he said, smiling at her goofily.

"Sir," Bethany replied with a friendly nod. "I was awake on a research project well past my bedtime and a little wine sounded good. As did the company. Hopefully, I'm not intruding?"

"You are not," Javier replied, trying to make heads or tails of what she'd just said. None of it sounded like Bethany. Presumably, she was up to something. Hopefully good. "Bethany Durbin, I'm not sure you've really met Kiliyn and Milya. Folks, this is the ship's Librarian."

Brinov checked her out like a fresh side of meat just arrived at the butcher. Kuzmandieva had a bit more jealousy in her eyes. Still, both smiled.

"Welcome," Brinov greeted her. "Why would a vessel like this need a formal Librarian?"

Those words were addressed to any of the three of them, but he figured Bethany was up to no good, so he'd let her explain.

"We have a *Sentience-in-Residence* aboard," Bethany explained carefully. As if that described his favoritest goofball.

"They have access to immense stores of information, but generally lack the training to curate it properly. As this voyage of discovery is taking us so far away from the nations of the distant east that we know so well, Captain Sokolov and the Ambassador determined that a Research Librarian would be a useful addition to the crew. My usual task is to locate more things for Suvi, then to help her place them within a context."

Javier smiled and took a drink. It all sounded perfectly plausible.

He knew better.

Bethany wouldn't have emerged to see her shadow unless she was after something. It would be intellectual. That was who she was.

"So you are after more than just trade, Javier?" Kiliyn asked, tearing his gaze away from Bethany.

"Much more," Javier replied breezily. "Information so that the next trade voyage might be much more profitable."

He didn't figure he'd be able to thread a camel through the eye of a needle either. At the same time, the galaxy might settle itself back down instead of firing up another war, in which case the Khatum might let him out to play some more.

And she might not.

"What information rates highest?" Milya asked, showing that she wasn't just another pretty face.

She was that, too. Average height. Above-average looks. Fantastic bottom. Brains, too, which moved her over into the category of sexy. Doubly so when you found out that she was a good conversationalist on a number of topics.

"This is an older stretch the colonized galaxy," Zakhar broke in now. "Depending, we might even make it to *Earth* on this voyage, but mostly we wanted to establish who among the old worlds was doing the best, and who might be faltering. Trade goes separate directions when that happens."

Javier would have sworn that both of the strangers jolted, ever so slightly, at what Zakhar said. Might be worth going back and asking Suvi to replay the tape later. She was monitoring everything, everywhere, though most of it got flushed out of memory in a day or three. Empty chambers making usual noises, and all that.

Didn't get his hackles up, but sure did blink his attention.

"What kind of trade?" Brinov asked now.

The man's tone had gone…*weird*. Javier didn't have a better term for it, as colorful as he could get when pressed.

"We've got a tremendous volume of space," Zakhar replied, gesturing to the ship with both arms. "Most of it currently unused because we are neither a warship in service nor a freighter hauling goods. Think of the boat as a yacht just cruising. Well enough armed to see off any pirates, but not following any particular circuit through space."

Again, that weird jolt. Javier wondered if he could talk these two into a poker game. He didn't need the money, being a kept man himself, but it would keep his skills sharp to clean them completely out.

They had some interesting tells, for supposedly innocent travelers.

"How about you?" Bethany the Librarian suddenly impersonated an extrovert. "What takes you to *Ormint*?"

It even sounded innocent, but Javier was too nice to take all of Bethany's money at a poker table. He'd leave that for Sascha and Hajna to do.

Man, this conversation was going to be weird if the two strangers kept acting like guilty teenagers caught sneaking out after dark. Milya had frozen. Kiliyn looked like someone had just prodded him in the kidneys with a knife.

Not that anyone had ever done that to Javier. No, sir. Innocent as driven snow.

"Exploring trade opportunities," Kiliyn managed awkwardly. "The two worlds do not have a lot of direct contact, so we thought to see what openings we might exploit."

"Interesting," Bethany said. "If you find yourself in need of the services of a librarian while we're still in-system, please don't hesitate to ask. I enjoy solving mysteries and finding things."

At this point, Javier was surprised that neither of the strangers physically levitated out of the booth like characters in a cartoon from the way they twitched.

"I think, however, the wine is catching up with me," Bethany continued. "Must have been more tired than I thought, so I'll bid you all a good night."

She rose, bowed, and withdrew.

Javier refrained from pointing out that she'd started with a short pour in a small glass and hardly had more than a mouthful since. The whole scene had fallen over like a bagpiper on a unicycle who'd had to sneeze suddenly.

Thankfully, both Kiliyn and Milya chose to flee from the field of battle immediately after Bethany vanished.

"That actually sounds wise," the man said, sliding out of the booth and straightening his blazer. "Shall we, my dear?"

Milya might have been shot out of a cannon, as fast as she moved.

Quickly, it was just him and Zakhar.

"That went...*interesting*," Zakhar observed.

"Bethany's up to something," Javier retorted.

"Duh?" Zakhar grinned. "However, I will remind you that you hired her. No way you're making me an accessory here."

Javier shrugged and finished his own glass. Cale looked up but Javier waved him off more wine.

Instead, he rose and stretched. Quiet sounded good, right about now, but he suspected that he wasn't going to bed anytime soon.

Not with whatever his favorite Librarian was up to.

PART FIVE

Bethany felt like a character in one of those vids that Suvi kept in the library to watch, solving crimes and *doing things*.

Her. The Librarian. The woman who had wanted nothing more than to work the stacks for a career, finding things for admirals and hardly ever emerging into the sunlight.

She'd hardly gotten to her cabin when a knock at the door almost caused her to scream.

Maybe a bit too wound up.

Bethany took several deep breaths and composed herself before opening the hatch.

Javier.

"Hi," she managed, but he just walked right by her into her front room and sat in a chair.

The man pointed at the couch.

"Sit," he ordered.

Bethany found the button to close the hatch on her second try and staggered bonelessly to collapse across from the man who'd offered her a life of adventure, were she only willing to take it.

Everything after that was probably her own damned fault.

"What do you know and what should I be prepared for?" he began without any preamble at all.

Of course, they'd both just come from—could you call it a confrontation when it went down like that?—an encounter in the Lounge.

"It's complicated?" she offered.

Javier laughed outright, which was just about the opposite of what she'd been expecting.

"Kid, easy gets boring," he said. "And you wouldn't need me playing straight man. What was up with our guests that you wanted to poke them?"

"Wasn't her, boss," Suvi suddenly descended from the heavens like a protecting angel, but Bethany knew that she needed to do more than let her partner-in-crime handle it.

"It wasn't just me," Bethany corrected. "Suvi saw something and needed some help figuring out what it meant."

"So talk," he said, leaning back.

"Brinov was wearing that weird brooch," Bethany said.

"David, yes," Javier nodded.

"So the stone across the chest is more than just a gem," Bethany said. "Suvi found something inside it."

"You talk," Javier interrupted when Bethany was all set to slide sideways out of the spotlight. "I'll ask her questions after that."

"She thinks it contains a map," Bethany said. "I'll let her explain that part. The other part was an ancient flag that her research suggests might be the symbol of a group of scientists that built themselves a giant ship and disappeared from Earth, intending to sail halfway around the galaxy or something before establishing a proper colony. This, back when such a trip would have taken maybe two decades to complete, with the primitive jumpdrives they had."

"Okay?"

He could be a pain in the ass when he got serious. She occasionally missed her old job, because right now he had a look like a grumpy admiral needing something that nobody had ever written down.

"At the same time, the technology to make the stone, according to Suvi, wasn't available to those folks," Bethany said. "Assuming they left around 5500, they'd have needed access to kit and tech comparable to ours today, after the big jump everyone got from the General War over the last century."

"Seriously?" Javier asked.

"Javier, the stone is much older than the brooch," Suvi spoke up. "At least a thousand years, though I would need a better scanner to nail it down. I could make it. You could probably program a machine to make it, but like I told Bethany, it would take you years. Even you."

"Okay, so boil it down," the man said. "Lost colony leaves behind a map? Is that the trail you're following?"

"Maybe," Bethany said. "I mean yes, that was what got her attention."

"And you?"

"I wanted to know if the man had any idea what the thing was that he was wearing," Bethany replied. "You and your trips to the pawn shops, everywhere that we go."

"Gotcha," he nodded. "Maybe someone else had it then lost it and he ended up with it because of the coolness factor."

"Exactly," Bethany said. "So I wanted to say a few things, just to see his reaction."

"Kid, I thought they were both going to have medical

events, sitting across from them," Javier laughed. "Based on what you'd said, and I will expect a full write-up at some point in the next thirty-six hours, they are hiding something big, and you accidentally stumbled over it."

"So what do we do about it?" Bethany asked.

"You? Nothing," Javier said. "Suvi."

"Present and accounted for," Suvi replied merrily.

"I need you to override your regular programming," Javier said with a grin. "Here's what I need you to do…"

PART SIX

"You can't be sure," Kiliyn said angrily. "She might have just come to chat because it would be rude to avoid the guests. Plus, she's a librarian, so perhaps she wanted to know more about us."

"That's what frightens me," Milya replied. "What if she does find out our secrets? We have waited a long time to be able to do this. Many people would kill to know the truths we hide."

"We don't know anything," Kiliyn snapped. "The whole point of this journey was to go to *Ormint* so we could find out what those people had recorded. Our early records on *Trotau Skale* are hardly worth mentioning, because everything was kept orally for so long. I think you are overreacting about the woman. She cannot possibly even guess at the truth."

"What if she is working for Belfast?" Milya asked now.

Kiliyn took a breath before he started yelling at the woman. Calm. Rational. Scientific.

As they aspired to being.

"The Belfast Group Holding Company are pirates," he reminded her. "We did much research on this vessel from its time at *Ugen*. They are also pirates, at least of a sort, but many of the crew members originally worked for the Jarre Foundation. All of them are now citizens of *Altai*. At the very least, their old Jarre connections would make them the enemies of Belfast. That was the only reason we could be sure that they would not tell Belfast. They have no reason. You are starting at ghosts."

"Those ghosts are millennia old," Milya said.

Still, she stepped back from confronting him now. Moved to the couch and settled, instead of the two of them standing just inside the hatch yelling at each other where someone in the corridor outside might hear something.

Kiliyn followed, taking the chair and stretching his legs out.

"We all know the old stories," he said, blowing out a heavy breath as he watched her also relax. "We were raised on them, after all. All of the old families were. It has taken this long before we were in a position to actually look into the truth of them. You know that."

"So you are saying we're being paranoid because we've always had to be?" she asked. "Is that it?"

"It has served us well for that millennia, Milya," he reminded her. "At *Ormint* we can find out more of the truth."

"Would we hire this ship?" she asked. "They are not Belfast."

"No, I agree with you there," he nodded sagely. "That conversation was odd, and we reacted poorly in our surprise. I think we should let them continue to *Earth*. Perhaps even steer them into that long of a trip. I expect that we would need to return to *Trotau Skale* with what we find, and then perhaps just buy our own ship and only bring as a crew those people initiated into the old mysteries. It is the only way to be certain."

"I saw you noticing the woman," Milya changed tack on him now. "She is certainly attractive. Would you bring her back to *Trotau Skale* and initiate her?"

Kiliyn glowered at his partner.

"You and I have no bond," he said slowly. "Anything with the woman would be purely physical, just as it would be if you continued to throw yourself at Sokolov or Aritza. And no, I would not let her know what we have hidden for so many generations. Not until she had spent a decade with us in ignorance, even as attractive as she is. The woman is too smart."

"We will need genes for intelligence," Milya noted. "The Clans have been extremely insular, save for bringing in occasional fresh blood, one way or the other."

"Feel free to get yourself impregnated by one of the men," Kiliyn half-snarled. "At least that child could be raised properly. I am taking no chances until we can determine the truth of Avalon and determine what our next steps are."

"You're right," she replied. "I am acting jealous, when I have no grounds. We are both free agents, assigned to this mission as a cover. Still, why don't you take me to bed and remind me why those pirates aren't worth pursuing…"

"That's it?" Javier asked.

"The important bits of the recording end at this point," Suvi replied with a verbal shrug. "From there, they fooled around on the couch for seventeen minutes before taking a shower together for another twenty-six, including some time spent fooling around with the water turned off to not have the tanks run cold suddenly at a climactic moment. Then they went to bed and engaged in activities even a psychologist would rate as pretty damned vanilla."

"They can't run out of hot water," Bethany said, confused. "Don't they know that?"

"I suspect that *Trotau Skale* is poor," Javier said. "Some of the things that Brinov said over dinner and afterwards lean towards a colony only a little better off than *Neu Berne*."

"But Djamila's people lost a major war and were taxed pretty heavily as punishment," Bethany cried. "What happened to the colony *Trotau Skale*?"

"That's going to be your job," Javier said.

"Mine?"

"We're going arrive at *Ormint* shortly," he said. "They wanted to research their own history, as well as *Ormint*. I suspect that they've lost some of the pieces they needed. Maybe they know there is a map in there, but need somebody as smart as an upgraded *Sentience* to read it."

"Upgraded?" Bethany asked.

"My cousins are dull and linear folks, Bethany," Suvi laughed now. "I'll blame Javier for everything he did to make me more like you than them."

"Guilty as charged," Javier laughed as well, turning to see the goofball's face on a nearby panel. "I needed better conversation than I could get from my various generations of chickens. That's what happens when you leave me alone with a toolkit and a computer."

"Is there likely to be such a machine at *Ormint*?" Bethany asked. "One good enough to tell them what's inside that stone without selling such information off to someone like Belfast. Hey, is Belfast a threat?"

"Dunno," Javier said. "My plan is to hassle Zakhar, Djamila, and Afia in the morning and see what they know."

"And then?" Bethany asked.

"And then maybe we go searching for buried treasure," Javier grinned.

PART SEVEN

A fia had learned not to trust that gleam in Javier's eyes. Man could talk you into just about anything when he had that smile going.

Afia could testify to that. Not that it would be bad. Heaven forbid. Javier never left a girl hanging. At the same time, you'd probably be asking yourself how you got into this particular mess.

Like now.

Breakfast. She'd awoken to a note from the man asking her to join him and the others a bit later than normal for her, so she'd hit the gym first, showered, and here she was, sitting in the main wardroom with Zakhar and the Dragoon.

And the troublemaker himself.

"I thought we weren't pirates anymore?" she asked, head tilted just that perfect amount to get his mouth pursed defensively. "You sure this doesn't cross some ethical line somewhere, such that we should consider stopping you now?"

Afia liked the grin that came over Djamila's face. The woman would enjoy doing that to Javier.

Unfortunately, she and the Captain seemed to be on Javier's side here, having heard the whole spiel.

"This isn't piracy," Zakhar chimed in, even before Javier could finish taking a drink of his coffee and winding himself up to bamboozle her some more.

"No?" Afia turned to the man.

The four of them really represented the power on this ship, plus Suvi listening in as she no-doubt was. Captain Sokolov. Djamila representing the Centurions. Javier representing the Khatum.

And sneaky, little Afia Burakgazi as Shop Steward, responsible for the union representing the rest of the crew. Kept her on her toes.

"So, let's assume that eavesdropping on our guests and Suvi scanning his butt don't cross that line," Zakhar began, only to be interrupted by his comm, currently resting face down on the table.

"I scan everybody," Suvi's muffled voice carried. "Most of you are boring."

Afia had to agree with a chuckle. Even the exciting parts of the last six years since they'd shanghaied Javier really only covered about three months, if you strung them all together. The rest was laundry, sleep, and meals for the most part.

"Given," Zakhar said, going so far as to flip the comm over face up so Suvi could officially be part of the conversation. Suvi's image ended up facing Afia. "Assuming additionally that the ship was built, and sailed, I have the impression that it was subsequently abandoned. At least that's how it sounds. If Javier and Bethany are right that maybe *Trotau Skale* was colonized by the descendants when something went wrong, we can also assume that they either parked the ship, like *Neu Berne* did with *Hammerfield*, or they put it on a specific course on a specific date, and we just have to track that."

"Why leave it in motion?" Afia asked. That part she didn't get.

"If you put it around a star, eventually somebody is going to find it," Zakhar smiled. "Maybe some isolated introvert on a *Concord* surveying contract or something equally silly and unbelievable."

Afia laughed when Javier actually blushed. He did that more than he used to. That was a good thing. Boy needed to relax.

"But flying?" Afia pressed.

She was an engineer, not a pilot. Her life was down aft with the power systems and Jumpdrives. Rarely did she see stars, except when her occasional job as a Combat EVA Specialist caused her to do things she didn't write home about.

"One percent of light speed is fast," Javier chimed in. "Thirty thousand kilometers per second, which sounds like a lot, until you remember that it takes you one hundred years to travel one light-year. If we take Brinov at face value, they're expecting that the ship was abandoned sometime around when *Trotau Skale* was founded. Ballpark that nine hundred and fifty years ago. The ship would have gone less than ten light-years in that time. Easy enough to scan all the vicinity as it existed in those days in order to find a hole to send a ship through safely. *Hammerfield* would have stayed stable for maybe two more centuries where we found it, before something came along and either knocked it into a planet or tossed it into deep space. Personally, I might have dropped that initial velocity back to one-tenth of a percent relative speed. So less than one light-year traveled."

"Second star to the left and straight on until morning?" Djamila asked with a twinkle in her eyes that matched Javier's now.

"This boy is no longer lost," Javier countered. "Maybe even growing up."

"But piracy?" Afia butted in.

"Suvi says the tech is way in advance of anything the galaxy should have had access to in those days," Javier replied, turning deadly serious now like he did when shit was about to go down. "Perhaps as good as we have today. Perhaps better?"

"You want to steal that," Afia said.

"There's that," Javier nodded. "At the same time, there is a war coming, Afia. The General War ended when *Neu Berne*, *Balustrade*, and the *Union of Man* exhausted themselves. The *Concord* kind of tipped the scales quietly, just because nobody wanted *Neu Berne* to win. So we've had peace now for ninety years or so. That is breaking down."

"Your *Rising Storm*," Afia said.

"Technically, the term originated with Dorn Hetzel, back on *Bryce*," Javier said. "He taught Political History to both me and Bethany, though he came along after Zakhar graduated. Dorn saw it coming. And last time I talked to him, which was two years ago now, he was writing a new book on the topic with better timelines after twenty-five years of research. I have a rough draft, prepublication, that I have been annotating and offering suggestions based on being out in the field, since Dorn is just a professor back safely behind lines."

"So *Altai* will have access to the tech?" Afia asked. "What about everybody else?"

"Who do you trust if we find a superweapon of some sort?" he asked her point blank.

Afia felt the other two stir uncomfortably.

There was ethics, and then there was playing God. Still, Javier had the most experience with that, having run the greatest scam in recent memory on the rest of them to be able to hide Suvi, then pour her into a warship of this power.

"Hell, we might not even tell the Khatum," Javier continued. "That's the sort of decision I expect the five of us to make, if and when we get there."

"Five?" Suvi asked, before Afia could.

"You'll outlive us all, kiddo," Javier turned to the comm. "You and your future generations will inherit whatever choice we make, long after any of us are in the grave and beyond hurting."

"But superweapons, Javier?" Suvi asked.

"If technology can make someone a god, that might go to their head, Suvi," he said with the sort of deadly serious intent that left Afia shivering inside. "You know how I feel about absolute power and incorruptibility. Maybe you'll need to have a weapon nobody but you knows about, on that day when it becomes necessary to kill a god. Then you'll be glad if you have such a thing handy."

Afia watched Javier suck all the heat, light, warmth, and humor out of the room like a black hole someone had just dumped in a punch bowl.

She still occasionally forgot about those sides of the man.

Mostly, you got the goof, the botanical nerd, and the poker player, but he was still as hard as any *Concord* officer she'd ever met. From the looks on the other three faces, they had forgotten, too, so she didn't feel so bad.

Afia took a deep breath.

"So piracy is a given?" she said. "As well as cat burglary, espionage, and god-slaying?"

"Nobody ever told you this job would be easy, Afia," he smiled grimly.

"Sometimes you gotta be heroes, too?" she said.

The four of them just nodded.

39

"So who's going with me to *Ormint* besides Bethany?" she asked.

"You aren't volunteering," Javier said.

"Why not?" Afia growled at him like the pixie grizzly her family had accused her of being.

"You all are known pirates," he said. "Even around here."

"So is Navarre," Zakhar pointed out dryly.

"I'm not Navarre," Javier countered.

"No?" Afia asked.

"Nope," he grinned. "Doctor Javier Eutrupio Aritza, lately of King's College. Here on a research project."

Afia made a sound that wasn't entirely rude, because he wasn't entirely wrong.

"You're going to need someone to handle cargo on the ground," she pointed out.

He grimaced, and the others smiled.

The stop at *Ormint* had just gotten longer and more interesting, though.

She wondered if she'd end up having to rescue him and Bethany at some point.

ORMINT

PART ONE

Bethany would have asked how she'd been roped into this, but that answer was obvious. Nobody but her had the grounding of context or the skill at research to do this thing.

Whatever this thing ended up being.

They'd gotten to *Ormint* without any more bizarro incidents. Brinov and Kuzmandieva hadn't said anything more incriminating after that one night. Maybe they had figured out that the ship itself was listening.

On the brighter side, everyone in the crew who knew the truth was smart enough to stay utterly silent on the topic of Brinov and anything that might be associated with the legend.

They were down on the flight deck today. Del had a petite passenger and cargo shuttle that he hated flying, but not enough to make Javier hire a second pilot for the ship.

You just got to listen to the man bitch. More than once, Bethany had turned on an audio recorder to catch some of his stories that came out when you got him to talking. Or asked Suvi to transcribe the tapes.

Nothing she would ever publish while Del was alive, but he was the only person on the crew who even approached Javier for the insanity of some of his adventures.

Like the Lander, the Shuttle had no name. Nothing painted on the side identifying it and perhaps marking it for the gods to take umbrage. Yet more of Del's stories, but she was as superstitious as the next sailor, so she didn't complain.

Anything that kept Del alive kept her safe too.

"Flight Control, this is Del," he said, when they were all settled in the passenger section. "Ready to launch. The station awake?"

Bethany contained her chuckles. That was Del. Brusque, sometimes to the point of rude.

As Javier said, it was a good thing he was the best pilot in the galaxy.

"You're green, Del," Suvi said on the intercom. "Rear doors opening now. Flight plan is filed and cleared by ground authorities."

Bethany looked around the space. Her and Javier. Afia in her new disguise handling cargo, which just happened to put her on the ground as an ambassador for Suvi, who really handled quartermaster duties.

Brinov and Kuzmandieva and their personal gear in two coffin-sized steamer trunks.

Nobody else.

Bethany wanted to shrug, but Javier was right. Most of the crew were known pirates. Even having Afia on the ground was a touch risky, but she'd been a nobody crew member, rather than one of the Centurions on the old ship *Storm Gauntlet*.

Even today, Afia wasn't an officer. Andreea Dalca was the Chief Engineer, but she never wanted to talk to anyone if she could avoid it. An introvert even worse than Bethany, which was interesting.

Afia was a Lead Engineer these days, but mostly she was a gopher who handled things, which was why she was the Shop Steward. Plus, she'd been there when Suvi'd been born, so to speak.

"Everyone grab your ass!" Del yelled from the front, powering things up.

You were supposed to emerge carefully from a landing bay. But then, pilots were supposed to do a lot of things carefully.

Most of them refused. Del had made an art form of denial.

Bethany had a view out the forward bay, so she saw the mouth as *Excalibur* regurgitated the shuttle. Then the sharp snap turnover that had the ship flying ass-first as Del engaged the thrusters to knock them out of orbit.

Nothing calm or measured, except that Del didn't have a single wasted motion.

The noise wasn't too bad, though Bethany knew it would be once they started biting atmosphere and riding in hot.

Because Del.

"So how long will you be on *Ormint*?" Bethany turned and called across the way to Brinov and Kuzmandieva. It might sound suspicious, but she was mostly curious.

Travelers represented information moving around, like Chaucer and his Canterbury Tales. Bethany always sought ways to capture that for some future researcher who might need to know.

"Perhaps a month," Brinov replied after a few seconds.

He seemed nervous, but that might just be Del's flying. You had to get used to it.

"After that, we will look to see what ships are headed to *Trotau Skale* that we might book passage on."

Bethany nodded. Javier had made it clear that *Excalibur* would be breaking orbit long before then, and possibly headed towards *Zyga's Landing*, which put them on a path to places like *New Angeles* or *Terra Nova*, the oldest and second oldest surviving colonies ever sent out.

Not all of them had survived. Terraforming in those days was much less of a science. Bethany had heard the stories from folks about *Svalbard*, which had been in the process of failing as a terraforming attempt. Even then, *Svalbard* would last for perhaps another ten or fifty thousand years as habitable for humans.

Just cold and miserable, anywhere outside of five degrees from the equator.

And they were looking for a colony that had never landed on a planet? Just a ship heading through the darkness forever like some Flying Dutchman?

Bethany's shudders weren't all from the bumpiness of Del's flight.

PART TWO

J avier waved at Kiliyn and Milya as they got focused on those big trunks. Powered rollers would help them move the beasts around, but they were still huge and heavy as they started to roll in the direction of ground transportation.

They were on the surface of *Ormint*. Main city: also *Ormint*. Out in the landing field for now, but Del wasn't going to be on the ground for long before departing.

Javier picked a different direction from his former guests and started walking, Bethany and Afia falling in with him.

For this mission, he'd brought a couple of suits in case he had to impress somebody. One had been tailored to make him look like an awkward academic, always a useful disguise. The other went with his title as Ambassador, in case one of the local politicians decided that maybe they needed a grip and grin session, possibly over rubbery chicken at some fundraising dinner.

Politicians were always raising money for something.

Most of the time he was on *Ormint*, Javier planned to

keep a low profile and hang out in libraries and book stores. Maybe some museums. The occasional coffee shop.

Vacation, as it were.

He didn't figure there would be much opportunity for fooling around, but he wasn't looking for it either. Bethany was too much an employee still. Afia was a little too wound up. Behnam was nearly a third of the way around the galactic rim.

He'd get by.

Javier turned to Afia now and smiled.

"I have your comm number, if we need you," he said simply. "You get supplies covered and then hide in the hotel until someone calls."

"Yes, Dad," Afia snarked at him.

"I'd rather you had to break me out of jail, Afia," Javier reminded her. "That's likely to just be petty theft and trespassing. Someone recognizes you and we have other troubles."

She sobered, which was his intent. Nodded.

"See ya soon," he said, turning again on a vector that would split off from her goal to visit some of the chandlery shops.

Ormint was pretty old. Mature, he supposed, as planets went. Occupied for something like three thousand years at this point. Old enough to have its own history, as it were.

Afia was on the ground because the prices for everything would be cheaper. Most folks didn't fly ships big enough to have their own shuttles for cargo, so they ended up docking at one of the stations overhead like pearls on a string. And paying captive prices.

Javier was too cheap. Plus, it would let them see the sights.

"Now what?" Bethany asked when the two of them were alone, headed towards the flight terminal.

The other thing Javier liked about *Ormint* was the lax attitude about travelers. He'd been places where everyone had to be scanned and fingerprinted on arrival. *Ormint* assumed that you had enough money to travel, and therefore didn't need the hassle.

"We've got reservations at a different hotel from the rest of them," he replied. "I figure if we disappear from history, as far as Kiliyn Brinov is concerned, they'll relax. They might even wait until we leave before they start doing any serious research of the sort you'll do as soon as we get settled. I want to be gone to our destination and handling it. Whatever it is. Utterly gone before they come looking, because I have no idea what kind of help they'll bring when they come."

"You assume they'll need help?" she asked.

"Poverty," Javier reminded her. "Even in an interstellar culture, you can be poor enough that you have to catch a ride on a ship going the right direction. I presume they have to do the same to get back to *Trotau Skale*. Then they have to outfit a ship to find their buried treasure."

"What kind of ship would that be?" she asked as they walked.

Bethany was in better shape than him, but that was her youth and all the time spent climbing ladders in stacks to get books. Emma St. Kitts, the Doctor of Sports Medicine half of the Drs. St. Kitts, had everyone doing more exercise these days. Martial arts. Strength training.

He could still out-run most of the crew in a marathon, but Bethany would be right in his pocket the whole time.

"Actually?" he asked. She nodded. "If we were completely innocent travelers and traders, I'm not sure you could find a better vessel than *Excalibur* with Suvi. She's trained as a cartographer and survey expert, and has sensors better than she did when she was a probe-cutter. I expect that our friends would end up having to hire something like that broken-down tub *Calypso*, back on *Svalbard*."

He noted her grimace, and understood. Even in the *Concord* Navy, richest in the sector these days, only the admirals rode in comfort. Everyone else was in a box with enough life support, engines, and jump drives to get around. Mostly.

"But we're not going to be hired by them?" Bethany confirmed.

"We'd have to turn pirate at that point," he assured her. "Take them captive after they got us there, and then you have the question of letting them go again later to swear out yet more arrest warrants, or hire ninjas and enemy pirates to chase us. Not like Walvisbaai Industrial wouldn't cut them a hell of a deal on an assassination contract, when someone mentioned who the target was."

"Good," Bethany said.

Javier nodded and they walked. She'd hired on because there hadn't been many options, but also because he'd promised her they were getting out of the pirate business.

And illegal salvage fell under an entirely different set of numbers in most legal codes.

PART THREE

B ethany was unused to travel. Wasn't entirely sure she liked it.

There, she was willing to admit it.

At the same time, Javier had gotten them rooms in a nice place downtown, not that far from the university for which the city was possibly best known. Nice rooms.

She had a view across a street at what she initially took for a park, until she realized that it was part of the campus of University at Landing, that being the name of the neighborhood itself.

Landing.

The colony was so old that they still called places *Landing.* They had done that a lot in the old days, naming it after the first place ships would touch down bearing colonists.

Bethany found herself standing in the window, just looking at the trees across the way. They'd arrived during a months-long summer break in this hemisphere. Trees hid most things from this elevation, but there were a number of buildings emerging from the green sea below her like islands.

For a long moment, she was home on *Bryce*, back in her own library.

Back when she'd still had a career in the *Concord* Navy ahead of her, before the most recent round of budget cuts saw her duty station gutted and largely eliminated. Some fool of a politician certain that just loading everything into an electronic datacore and putting a *Sentience* in charge would result in sufficient cost-savings to justify the work.

Having met Suvi and spent so many months around the woman, Bethany could see what a stupid idea that was. Suvi might have what it took to be a competent librarian, in another few years. Most of them were designed and programmed to handle warships.

They didn't have Javier teaching them to be human.

Like he was doing to her, too.

Could she say that? Bethany wasn't sure. Certainly, she'd never tell him. Like Suvi, the man was something of a father figure these days. Maybe a revered uncle that was something of a black sheep to the rest of the family? Zakhar Sokolov played the grand, terrible Patriarch quite well.

At the same time, Bethany didn't want to think of Javier as family. She knew he had physical relationships with many of the women aboard ship, excluding Djamila pointedly from all the stories she'd heard.

Did she want that?

No. Not today at least.

Bethany wasn't sure what she wanted, and therein lay the crux of things.

Her original life plans had been tossed out the window. Demobilized as well as defenestrated, as it were. Maybe she'd have ended up taking that job as a waitress somewhere, just because there were far more librarians than jobs for them, and the Navy had just added a bunch to the job market.

Until Javier came along.

Dorn had called her an unbloomed rose. There was a kernel of truth there, as well. *Ugen* had taught her that life was cheap, in the grand scheme of things. With *Ugen* and the Navy, not even tomorrow was guaranteed, so you best grab life by the jugular right now and live it as hard and as much as you could.

Regrets were the mistake.

Yes, that was it. Regrets at things not done. Ideas left on the table because you never made time for them.

That was what she didn't want.

Bethany ignored her big bag and grabbed the satchel that contained her reader, some book chips, and a few sundries as she headed out the door. She considered her next step, changing her mind several times until she found herself knocking on Javier's door.

He opened quickly.

"What's up?" he asked.

"Put your shoes on," she ordered him. "I need to take a long walk around town and want a bodyguard along so I'm not worried about strangers."

"There might be a mob of them," he offered, stepping back and slipping a foot into a boot.

"If you think I should have Del bring Djamila down, just let me know," she smiled sweetly.

Low blow, but hey, Javier brought these things upon himself.

He grinned at the trap she'd walked him into and grabbed a light jacket as he stood up.

That sounded like a good idea, so she doubled back and got hers from her room before they took the lift to the ground.

"Anywhere in particular?" he asked, falling into step beside her.

"The campus," Bethany replied, letting her subconscious

be her guide right now. "Maybe food in a few hours."

She glanced up and did some quick math. Early afternoon, not that long after local lunchtime, regardless of her personal clock. Summer, so it would be warm but not that hot. The jackets would be useful later, after the sun went down, but breathed enough for now.

Bethany reached into her satchel and pulled out a stunner that she stuffed into her pocket. It had traveled with her to Jackson's Crossing, and everywhere beyond.

"We going looking for trouble?" Javier asked pointedly as she did.

"Looking?" Bethany grinned. "No, but you never know who you might meet on a train platform."

Like the first time she had encountered the pirate Navarre, who was really Javier pretending to be who he used to be, before Behnam.

"Very funny," Javier replied.

Bethany crossed the street at a corner, as traffic on the ground was a bit heavy. Fliers around here had to come in high, and then drop straight down to land. Safer. Doubly so if you let the autopilot handle it. So a lot of ground traffic.

Bethany didn't want autopilot in her life.

From below, the campus looked like home. She didn't do botany, but had an expert walking next to her if she wanted to know the species. They had all come from *Earth* originally, but not so long ago that they were new species. Probably.

She honestly didn't know if the terraforming process involved customizing the genes of the plants for a world. For a moment, she found herself reaching for her bag to pull out the machine that could answer anything before she stopped herself.

Bethany wanted to experience the galaxy, not just read about it. She walked.

At the center of a quad, she found a map station, a

wooden wall with a diagram at the center and then hundreds of advertisements and flyers tacked or glued around it, offering tutoring, companionship, gaming buddies, or bands recruiting members.

Excalibur didn't have live music. It had two expert composers who worked primarily in symphonies. Bethany grabbed one of the concert announcements that caught her eye and headed deeper in.

"Anything in particular?" Javier asked as they walked.

He'd offered no advice. No commentary. Nothing. Just walked along beside her like a date, though they weren't holding hands.

She considered it, just to give off a different image, but then wondered if she might meet any cute boys or girls at a show. Javier didn't act his age, but he'd still been born in '45, while she hadn't come along until '61. She was twenty-seven, going on sixty, as her mother would have said.

Tonight, she needed to have a little fun.

PART FOUR

Javier had followed Bethany for more than an hour as she meandered. Sauntered, as it were, like the old pilgrims walking to the Holy Land at their own pace. In between buildings, around parkways, under trees, through arcades.

The campus was huge, no question about it. Three kilometers on a side, with better than half of it some level of park and greenery. Buildings tended to reflect recent architectural trends, with only a few that looked ancient.

He reached out a hand as he stopped, grabbing Bethany's elbow and eliciting a surprised squawk.

The English Department was in this building, along with a few others.

"Here," he said, turning and walking towards the door.

"What…?" she started to ask, but was talking to his back.

He heard her quick-step to catch up.

Javier was at the front desk, pulling out a business card for the pretty coed behind the counter when Bethany arrived, so she just watched.

"Hiya," he said to the brunette young enough to be his

daughter and handing her his card. "Traveling academic. I don't have an appointment. Didn't even know we'd stop on this planet as we went by. Hoping you might have an expert in historical mythologies that hasn't taken the summer off, from whom I might ask some questions."

He smiled. The girl smiled back, but didn't process things quickly. Summer break and all that. Student on a job instead of professional.

"Dr. Javier Aritza, King's College, *Altai*?" she asked, reading the card he'd brought.

Fantastic for bamboozling folks. You'd never look for a hard-ass pirate named Navarre to be hiding as a professor.

"That's right," Javier nodded. "We're on something of a trade mission from that sector, but I'm following something up on my personal time while the ship in orbit deals with supplies and such."

Part of the reason he liked having Zakhar around. The man was perfect as a captain of a traveling warship who would take no shit from you. Left Javier lots of margins to color outside of.

"Historical mythologies?" the girl asked now.

"Legends originating in the colonization of space," Bethany spoke up now. "As opposed to fairy tales from ancient *Earth*. Modern incarnations of the flying Dutchman and things like that."

"Oh!" the young woman brightened. "That would probably be Dr. Askvig. I think he's in today. Shall I ring him?"

"If you can direct us, it would be easier to explain in person," Javier smiled.

He was of the age when most pretty young women like this one saw him as *old*, which hurt a little, but he could at least be charming about it. They'd all figure it out soon enough.

"Fourth floor," she said.

"Good," Javier nodded. "You keep the card and mark it in your register, in case someone asks who is wandering around when I get lost upstairs? Thank you."

And he was off. Took the stairs because the gravity around here was lighter than he was used to, and Emma St. Kitts had everyone running up and down stairs regularly to keep in shape.

"You couldn't get lost drunk," Bethany muttered from behind him as they got into the stairwell and ascended.

"She doesn't know that," he laughed. "And it gives me a cover if we do have to scout around."

"What are we up to?" Bethany asked.

He grinned. *We.*

For a young woman who hadn't wanted to be a pirate when she grew up, Bethany Durbin was doing a pretty good job of it.

"I figure that a ship like that might leave behind memories," Javier said. "Your flying Dutchman reference is probably the closest."

"Will we leave memories behind, if they come this way?" she asked now.

"Probably," Javier agreed. "But I intend to get gone pretty quickly. If nothing else, we have a map that should get us close and I know a woman who's pretty damned good at survey work."

"Then why bother?" Bethany followed up. "I mean, I am all for more information. However…"

"Why did they abandon it, if they did?" Javier asked. "What did they leave behind? *Did* they abandon it, or are we only hearing the story of a group of disgruntled rebels who split off from the main group? Lots of things up in the air that we might trace. I'd rather not be surprised."

"Gotcha," Bethany said.

They emerged onto four and Javier quickly oriented himself.

Academia was the same it had always been. Small offices crammed with books around a single desk, even in an age when everything could be electronic.

He still loved the feel and smell of a real book, printed on paper with ink rather than plastic. Something about it grounded him in ways no other option could begin to approach.

Office hours. Students come by to complain about a grade or inquire about extra credit. Most of the offices were closed. Folks in summer hiatus, he supposed, as opposed to taking the time to finish the next book.

After realizing he had no more future in the *Concord* Navy, this had been a track he could have pursued all those years ago. Would have driven him even crazier.

Part of the reason he bought an old survey-probe and loaded it up with chickens. Not that they were any less fractious than academics, but he could ignore the cluckers and lock them back in the botany station when they got pissy.

Javier counted numbers to his left and found the office he wanted.

"Dr. Askvig?" he presumed, stepping to but not into the doorway itself.

Wizened little gnome of a man. Late fifties or well-preserved sixties. Bad suit. Like someone had picked one out when he was eighteen and he'd purchased exact replicas ever since. Might have worked had he hired a tailor to fit it better. Javier had such people on the ship for exactly that reason.

The man behind his desk had been working on a manuscript. Every professor was forever working on something he or she needed to publish. You had to. Part of the job requirement. Even Dorn had published a number of articles on his *Rising Storm* theory over the years, just to keep the Department Chair off his butt.

Askvig looked up with a fussy smile. Prim and authoritative.

"Dr. Aritza?" he asked, confirming that the girl had called ahead to warn the man.

Not that Javier was surprised. He might have gamed it out that way when he stepped in the door of the building. And left his card with her.

"That's right," Javier nodded companionably, stepping now to and over the threshold. "My assistant, Bethany Durbin, is a trained Research Librarian from *Bryce* originally."

He reached out and pulled her into the doorway. A bit awkwardly. She was used to staying out of the way of Captains and Admirals. Men and women with real power, rather than small-minded academic chumps exercising vendettas over the coffee machine.

Not that he had strong opinions on the topic, or anything like that.

"What exactly were you looking for, Dr. Aritza?" the gnome asked now.

Javier took the opportunity to step fully into the office, resting his weight on the back of a chair loaded with more books. The room was crowded, but not hostile. Just full of books, in a good way.

"We're from a much younger sector of space," Javier began spinning his yarn. He'd had a lot of practice on this one. "*Altai* is only about six hundred years old as a colony now, and still one of the oldest over yonder. I've been traveling as a designated Ambassador for the Khatum of *Altai*, looking to establish trade relations and Silk Road kinds of connections into this area. Most recently, we came from *Ugen* by way of *Trotau Skale*."

Javier liked the way the little gnome's eyes lit up at the mention of Brinov's home.

"*Trotau Skale*?" the man confirmed.

"Indeed," Javier agreed negligently. "An interesting place, but extremely young, as colonies go. We're more interested in some of the older ones, because of the connections to the early exploration era. As I said, trade, but we want to find those core worlds that tend to anchor social and economic networks, so that we find the strongest trading partners for our return voyage."

"You have a vessel capable of carrying trade that far?" Askvig perked up now.

Even in the current era, First Rate Galleons like *Excalibur* were exceedingly rare. It was an age of specialization for now. Dedicated warships and massive cargo beasts, rather than generalist craft that could do a little of everything.

The old *Hammerfield* hadn't quite been the last of her kind, but only a handful in that style had ever been made after she launched. Partly, *Neu Berne* losing the war had wrongly convinced people that the design must have some flaw.

It did, but only in certain kinds of warfare, as Javier didn't know any other ships of a comparable size that could haul a full crew like he had this far around the curve of the galaxy without having to stop to take on supplies constantly.

"We do," Javier replied, hoping that news of his various adventures hadn't really made it this far, lurid though they may be. "But I'm more interested in archaeology in your neck of the woods."

"Such as?" the man bristled a little.

"If I knew, I'd know," Javier said, pointing now. "I have a professional librarian on staff to abet my curiosity, but don't know where to aim her. What interesting stories might turn out to be good tourist traps I should go visit before returning home?"

In ancient times, every fool coming into the Levant had gone home with nails or shards from the True Cross. Or bones of famous saints that probably came from potter fields instead.

Not that the ancient saints hadn't most of them ended up thus, but Javier doubted that con artists would get that deeply into their research when they had suckers with gold at hand.

He could play such games with Askvig.

"We mentioned the ancient legend of the Flying Dutchman, on *Earth*," Bethany said now, twisting the conversation around in a new direction. "Ancient ships lost in space. Perhaps colonies that failed after a time and were abandoned? What interesting relics of the past might be out there, if you had a wealthy backer willing to send you halfway around the galaxy with spare time on your hands?"

Man, that woman played mean. Javier didn't have a better term to describe it. No university department ever had enough money for what they wanted to do. Professors were forever writing grant proposals to friendly but underfunded governments to supplement meager allotments.

Dangling gold in front of the man was like handing a drunk a half-empty bottle.

"There are many such in this sector," Askvig replied, relaxing in such a way that Bethany stepped fully into the room now.

Javier leaned on a vertical part of a bookshelf to look relaxed and out of the way. The gnome was seeing her as a student now, rather than a peer. He could understand why, as she didn't really look her actual age. Too many years in the shadows of a library, instead of out in the sun.

Being out of uniform, she might pass for an upperclass member if she did her hair right.

It was only when she started talking that you'd realize just how smart the woman was. There were a lot of reasons he'd hired her, after all.

"What's the most famous, Professor?" Bethany asked, eyes wide with interest and excitement.

She might have spent too much time around him and the crew, from the way she'd learned to act all innocent and helpful, getting the man to fill in all those details automatically.

"Hmmm…" the man contemplated. "If I had to guess, I would say *Kimmeria*."

Javier blinked. Not one he'd ever even heard of.

"Colony?" Bethany asked, understanding that she was going to get more mileage from the old fart than he was.

At least until they flip-flopped on the game of Good Cop/Bad Cop.

"Ship," Askvig replied. "Rather famous in this sector, though I am not surprised that such knowledge would not have made it far. It was something of a failure, supposedly abandoned in space."

Javier played a lot of poker with the crew. It kept his nerves sharp and his eyes innocent.

This sounded a whole bunch like another rumor he'd been pursuing.

Was it all just a pig in a poke? Was he a wanderer headed to the Holy Land, and Askvig another con artist? That didn't feel right, if for no other reason than Javier was really good at sniffing out such games.

He'd played enough of them over the decades.

"Where did it come from?" Bethany asked. "And if it was abandoned, where did the crew migrate to?"

"It came from *Earth* directly," Askvig nodded. "This

sector was the first place seriously colonized once safe and efficient star drives were built. Many worlds had been colonized, but had to be terraformed during settlement, rather than before. The latter happened around here. Bacteria. Insects. A full life cycle established, as an expert botanist would understand."

"Indeed," Javier nodded. "It wasn't until the Seedships were standardized that such things were possible, leading to the first twenty or so such colonies in this direction. But if the ship was abandoned, where did the people go?"

He held his breath as Askvig's eyes got narrow. Javier wondered if he'd just stepped into a minefield. Or rather, what kind.

"You are serious?" he asked sharply, leading Javier to wonder if the subject was one on which the professor got mocked, instead of respected. It had that kind of feel.

And it gave him an opening.

"My own vessel is an old First Rate Galleon that we salvaged from her celestial graveyard," Javier replied, willing to go out on a limb now to build some level of empathy with the man.

Something had just happened, but Javier didn't understand what it was that had set the man off.

"A First Rate Galleon?" Askvig gasped. "From the General War era?"

As far as Javier knew, the war had never really intruded this far west as anything more than a footnote. Most of the *Concord* had been in the way, and most of the war had happened well beyond the far borders of the *Concord*.

"Just so," Javier said. "It had been put into a complicated orbit in an obscure system two generations ago and lost until I stumbled upon it in my own explorations. You might say I have a thing for lost starships that might be recoverable."

"Which vessel?" Askvig's tone turned sharp. "Only a

handful were ever marked lost. I am unaware of any that were subsequently found."

"You know the history of the Great War?" Javier asked, suddenly confronted with another nerd like himself.

The galaxy might not be safe from their shenanigans, when you tossed in Bethany. She probably wouldn't appreciate having to babysit them as the only adult in the room.

"Stellar Mythologies, Aritza," Askvig replied. "Some of the greatest legends told originate from that time and space. I have published four tomes on them, two touching on that war. Behind you. Third shelf."

Javier turned and located the books. University at Landing Press, which didn't surprise him one bit. Nikos Askvig, PhD. Better author photo on the dust jacket than Javier would have expected. Must have brought in a pro.

He flipped to the table of contents and scanned the stuff. Yup, he was absolutely in the right place. Frighteningly right, considering how vague his questions had been. Askvig might have ended up in the History Department at a smaller school, except that he was focusing on the mythologies that emerge from space travel and wars, rather than the cold, dry dates of things themselves.

The lies we tell about ourselves that in turn get told to others as tall tales. Before they accidentally become history, when told third-hand.

Not that Javier Aritza had any experience with galaxy-shaking events.

Eutropio Navarre, now that was a different story.

Again, time to gamble. He turned to the wizened gnome and smiled.

"My ship?" Javier asked. "*Hammerfield*."

Shit, did the man just faint?

PART FIVE

Bethany wanted to say something, but this was Javier's game, so she sat and watched him and Askvig go back and forth. Still, it appeared that they'd managed to walk in the right door on the right day.

How much history of the galaxy was written the way it was because of such fortuitous circumstances?

"Professor, are you all right?" she asked now, watching the man perilously close to hyperventilating.

"*Hammerfield?*" he gasped.

Bethany was surprised that the man even knew the name, except that, like the *Excalibur* it had become, the myth of the lost warship was right up with King Arthur these days. Gone off to Avalon, to return in England's day of need. Or *Neu Berne's*.

In this case, Bethany had read some of the logs that Suvi had translated. The *Sentience-in-Residence* had suffered a malfunction somewhere that turned the mightiest ship built during the war into a coward that ran away and refused all orders to return. The crew had been trapped aboard, surviving every ambush or booby trap the stupid ship *Sentience* could play to kill anyone trying to get to it.

The crew had had no choice, as the ship would have killed them all eventually, so they killed it first. Then repaired the ship against the day it was ever found again, had themselves a final supper, and all went to their deaths by self-poisoning.

Not quite a Viking funeral, but not far off.

"*Hammerfield*," Javier confirmed.

Bethany wondered if the authorities had any arrest and extradition warrants handy, after what the rest of the crew of the newly renamed *Excalibur* had done since recovering the ship. Not that Walvisbaai Industrial didn't have it coming, according to what she'd read, but even the *Concord* had gotten concerned enough that Javier had taken the ship long ways around the curve of the galaxy, beyond even a hegemonic power like that one's reach.

Hopefully.

"Young man, do you have any idea what you've done?" Askvig asked.

"More than you probably imagine, Doctor," Javier replied. "I supplied the new *Sentience-in-Residence* aboard the ship. My old probe-cutter's crew. But that's a long story for another day. What about *Kimmeria*?"

Bethany was already mentally taking notes about spelling, linguistic drift, and such. The name sounded vaguely Russian or Turkish, depending on spelling. Languages used to change more frequently in ancient times when everything was oral. Now that it was written and electronically transmitted as video and audio files, things had not quite stabilized, but she could read most of the languages that had gone into interstellar space three thousand years ago.

Bethany stepped forward now, drawing Askvig's eyes to hers by squatting down to eyeball level with him.

"Professor?" she smiled charmingly. "*Kimmeria?*"

That seemed to break him out of his trance. He took a deep breath and leaned back now, blinking too rapidly but at least settling. It wasn't any worse than an Admiral you have to come back to, when some book they demanded doesn't even exist in the library, either because they've remembered it wrong, or saw it someplace like *Balustrade* or equally distant and a bit unfriendly spot.

Askvig sighed.

"Until *Hammerfield*, *Kimmeria* might have been the single most famous flying Dutchman in the sector, young lady," he said, blinking again and finding himself. "Scholar Durbin."

She nodded and smiled. The man had just promoted her in his own mind. That would help remarkably.

"Tell me how it came to be lost," she commanded lightly.

"Actually," Javier broke in now. "It's mid-afternoon. Professor, could we treat you to dinner someplace nice and expensive, as a way of thanking you for helping us?"

Bethany smiled. If nothing else, the Khatum had given Javier a big budget for entertaining, understanding that wine and good food loosened people up to talk trade and make deals.

And the rising storm was cutting into everybody's budgets for all the wrong reasons at all the wrong times.

"Well, there is the faculty club..." Askvig began, but Javier interrupted.

"I'm thinking a kilo and a half of prime rib," he said. "Smothered in butter and some local sauce. A couple of bottles of wine. Fresh sourdough bread. My treat. You pick the place. And is there a Mrs. Doctor Askvig we should be inviting?"

"Doctor Mrs. Askvig," the man corrected automatically, so Bethany assumed his wife was in the department somewhere, or a related one. History or Philosophy, maybe.

Close, but not immediately adjacent.

"Yes," the professor said after a beat. "Let me contact her."

Bethany rose and turned, nodding Javier to slip back into the hallway ahead of her to give the man a modicum of privacy.

"Thoughts?" Javier asked as the professor began chatting on a local comm with presumably the missus.

"He's likely to want to tour *Excalibur*," Bethany said. "You might have just triggered his next book. Especially after he meets Suvi."

"As long as you and I are the only points of contact," Javier nodded. "That way none of the other crew members let him connect the rest of the dots on what we did until we're gone."

"What if he wants to fly with us to find *Kimmeria*?" Bethany asked.

Javier grimaced.

"I thought so," she said. "You should put that in your back pocket against need."

She turned back to the Professor in his office as the man ended his call. Askvig smiled at them like the cat who had just eaten the canary.

PART SIX

J avier understood that a quick bribe to the manager of a nice place almost always managed to free up a table when you didn't have a reservation. Worked here, too.

Snazzy joint. Old school, with ceilings that looked like a second floor had been removed at some point. Or perhaps it had originally been a vehicle parking lot that had been enclosed to make a restaurant.

Carpet underfoot deep enough to quicksand you. Beige everything in a way that just calmed the nerves and seemed to vanilla your life.

He didn't do vanilla, but understood that other people would find that it helped with their digestion.

Doctor Mrs. Askvig turned out to be another cheery gnome like her husband. Growing old and starting to look like each other, as it were. Dressed just as fussily, and just as far out of sleek and stylish, though in her case the jacket looked handmade. By whom Javier didn't inquire.

Weird people. Even by his standards.

They were in the back of that vast, parking garage-looking main room. Beige linen tablecloth that covered the table to the floor and matched padded chairs. Pretty floral centerpiece that he figured was an odd mutant of a daisy, to get that same beige coloring. Assuming they weren't just hand-dipped. Or made of spun sugar.

Javier didn't feel like biting one to test.

Over-tipping the waitress as they sat down had gotten the woman's attention. The bill he'd slipped her probably matched what she made on a good night, all by itself. If he liked dinner, Javier would match it.

Red wine, because steak. He wasn't one of those purists that demanded his meat come from a cow instead of a vat, but he also wasn't about to live his entire life only eating vegetables and fruit.

Food got ordered and the waitress had an extra smile for him. Good to know he wasn't completely invisible these days.

Everyone was settled. Bethany was slowly noshing on a hunk of sourdough good enough that Javier considered asking for a bit of the starter to haul back to the ship at some point.

The Askvigs sat across from each other, so he had Nikos on his left.

"So here we are, and thank you again for offering, Dr. Aritza," Nikos nodded with a genuine smile.

Javier understood. Academics had job security, but the job never paid for shit.

"So we were talking about *Kimmeria*," Javier nodded back. "It is not a name I recognize, so perhaps you could fill in some of the background?"

"As with other flying Dutchmen, the legend has perhaps grown far beyond the truth," Nikos replied, grabbing his wine and taking a sip.

Good vintage. There was a reason you just bribed folks up front. Either you were planning to be an asshole and make a scene, or you wanted to put them at ease and encourage them to take extra special care of you.

Javier had learned the old adage about catching more flies with honey than vinegar and taken it to heart.

"Start with the legend, then, Professor," Bethany prompted.

"This is all third- and fourth-hand, mind you," he said, to which Javier nodded. "A group of scientists set out to build themselves an ark and sail a vast, perhaps impossible distance from *Earth*. Far beyond what the terraforming ships or the seedships of the era would be capable of achieving. Perhaps a distance as great as *Altai*, as our technology today is so much better and more robust than they had access to."

"Did they succeed?" Javier asked, glancing over at Leonora Askvig as well. She taught in the history department, though she hadn't said much so far.

"We do not believe so," Nikos replied. "Subsequent stories bear all the hallmarks of magic djinni, with the fabulous technology they supposedly already had, plus what they invented on their journey. We do know that the ship was supposedly abandoned later. Rumors suggest that some of the survivors made their way to *Trotau Skale*, but nobody has ever been located on that planet that would admit to knowing anything."

"*Trotau Skale*?" Bethany asked, trying to keep her face calm. They'd just come from *Trotau Skale*, and brought some folks with them, but neither of them had wanted to tell the two scholars that. "What kind of culture do they have?"

"An odd one, Scholar Durbin," he said, turning to her. Javier could see the fire of intellectualism take root in the man's eyes. "Insular to a degree that frequently reminds me of small fishing villages. Or perhaps asteroid miners. If you are an outsider, few people will talk to you, and there are no such stories told."

"Then what rumors pointed you there?" Javier asked.

So far, it sounded an awful lot like his previous guests, and he knew they were up to no good.

"Stories that traveled as far as *Ormint*," Nikos said. "They got written down here, but my attempts to follow up have always hit a dead-end."

"How old are the two colonies?" Bethany asked.

"*Ormint* is one of the oldest," Leonora spoke up now. She had a good speaking voice. Probably used to convincing stubborn minds to learn something in spite of themselves. Javier had known a few like that. "*Trotau Skale*, conversely, is the youngest, not counting a few mining colonies and such where a planet might be inhabited for a lifetime and not much longer."

"So…?" Javier led.

"*Ormint* will celebrate its third millennium in forty-six years," Leonora smiled. "I believe that *Trotau Skale* is approaching one thousand years since their founding."

"How old are the stories of *Kimmeria*?" Javier pressed now, fairly certain he was on the right path.

Whatever path it was.

"About the same age," Nikos nodded, eyes twinkling. "We think that most of the settlers went there, but a few subsequently chose to remove themselves to other planets. Political differences related to the failure of the ship, as it were. Recriminations. That sort of thing."

"How long were they in space, then?" Bethany asked.

Javier wondered if you could really build a generational ship. Either you needed to tinker with genetics to have humans who lived far longer than normal, or you'd be turning over your crew pretty regularly.

Eventually, you'd have kids like him come along. Good-time-folks rather than serious scholars and engineers. Javier was reasonably certain that any career he'd have chosen at eighteen would have been wrong. He'd joined the Navy because that was what you did in his family. Both parents. Three uncles and one aunt. Both sets of grandparents.

Permanently locked in a sealed environment, he'd have become a hoodlum.

Javier wondered if they would have allowed someone like him to actually grow up, or arranged for him to not be a burden on a closed society.

Had that been the problem?

Philosophers sometimes called it the grandchildren problem. The founding generation of any grand experiment were the deeply committed. The hard-ass types, willing to make any sacrifice to achieve their goal.

Their children would be young when the founding occurred, and possibly know some level of hardship that would shape and hone them, helping cement their loyalty.

The grandchildren, however, would be raised in a place where the struggles of the elderly were slowly being forgotten. Especially if the founders were successful. They'd grow up coddled by money and power, most likely. Never having wanted for anything in their life.

Soft. In a bad way.

The *Concord* Navy made hard-asses of you. Strict discipline designed to break a goofball down and slot him into his place. Line Command, with a background in hard sciences.

It had even worked for a while.

Until his grief, irrepressibility, and substance abuse issues had flamed him out.

Multiply that by an entire culture, and the outcomes were probably similar. Might take longer. Probably still happened on a timescale a sociologist could predict with reasonable accuracy.

He held his counsel. Kept his cards close to the vest, as it were.

"How long were they in space?" Nikos replied to Bethany's original question after a pause of contemplation. "It is hard to tell."

"What he means is that Nikos has several sets of stories, most of which disagree with each other, and none of them grounded in anything remotely scientific," Leonora said with a grin that made her look much younger.

Obviously a running joke in the family, from the way Nikos smiled back at her.

"Option one, they survived for only a few centuries on the ship, before putting it into orbit somewhere," Nikos continued. "Later, the colony failed, so they all emigrated elsewhere. *Trotau Skale*, for example. Sometimes the terraforming does not take."

"I have been a few places like that," Javier said, without offering any more evidence of previous criminality.

"Just so," Nikos said. "Option two, they moved slowly from *Earth*, as one might if you didn't have a particular destination. Perhaps they had found a spot in deep space, well away from any planets. Or found a star without a planetary disk and orbited it for a time."

"What's the weirdest theory?" Javier asked.

"That they had circumnavigated the entire galaxy over a course of one thousand years, and were almost back to *Earth* when something broke down and they had to abandon ship in a hurry," Nikos said. "Thus, survivors mostly alighted on *Trotau Skale*, but don't talk to outsiders because they were almost an alien species now, at least at the time. The colony has turned into a poor, boring place. Usually, those are the ones that have stories indicating that they were much mightier once, but angered the gods or something, and were thus cast down from the heavens."

"You are taking this remarkably well," Leonora broke in now. "Most folks scoff at such tales, or at least lose interest. You have not. Why is that?"

Bethany was hiding her grin behind the next piece of that excellent bread. Javier caught motion out of the corner of his eye indicating that dinner would be arriving in about twenty seconds.

Did he ignore the question and hope she would forget it later? Leonora Askvig didn't look like that kind of person. Nor did Nikos.

Bethany would be no help because this was his mission. His ship. His curiosity, even.

His execution.

Still, all this had been speculation until now, except for the parts where a random stranger held pieces of a puzzle Javier hadn't even known existed two weeks ago.

He turned to Nikos first, then Leonora. It had been her question, as her husband wasn't aggressive enough to force the issue. At least that was the impression he gave off.

"The circumnavigation theory is wrong," Javier said simply.

Leonora's eyes blinked too many times. Nikos's mouth fell open.

"We think we have a map that shows where the ship went," Javier said, gambling now.

Except that he rarely gambled. Poker was a game of social interaction. Learning the other players and being able to step back when they drew a winning hand, as well as go for the throat when they were bluffing.

He wasn't bluffing.

"A m-m-map?" Nikos stammered. "*Kimmeria?*"

"We don't know," Javier said. "My plan is to see what's there. It being summer break, perhaps the two of you might be interested in providing your expertise as part of a short sail?"

"Short?" Leonora poked.

"Within this sector," Javier said. "My ship has a *Sentience-in-Residence* that is better than just about anybody else. And an expert surveyor, from my time flying survey contracts for the *Concord* Navy. I have a pretty good idea where to look."

"What do you expect to find there?" Nikos asked in a voice filled with dread.

Bethany was grinning, so Javier nodded to her to tell them.

She was the Scholar, after all. She would work with the two Askvigs as they got closer.

"Buried treasure," Bethany smiled. "The best kind."

EXCALIBUR

PART ONE

Zakhar wanted to glower at the man. Bethany sitting next to Javier wouldn't protect the Ambassador from getting his ass chewed out, but Zakhar understood that this was one of those situations where everyone had gone off the reservation a little.

Not that this crew weren't experts at that sort of thing. Life of piracy, and all that.

Still…

"It's not the dumbest thing I've ever heard come out of your mouth," Zakhar said. "I will give you that much. Hell, not even the worst this week. Not sure that makes it a good idea."

Bethany had the courtesy to look chagrined. She was still too used to the uniform, and the green Zakhar habitually wore was close enough in color.

Javier just grinned.

"Shell game," he said, as if that explained it all.

Zakhar scowled.

"Fine," Javier said with a deeply put-upon sigh, like a cat Zakhar had kept as a mouser on a previous ship. "It's like this: I need to get the information out of his head, and we don't have time to track down copies of all his books, assimilate them, and then form a theory that helps. Too much gray area left on the map."

"So you invited him and his wife to join us?" Zakhar asked.

"He is, by his own admission, the most knowledgeable expert on the topic," Javier replied. "I have no idea who Brinov and his girlfriend were planning to talk to, but doing it this way takes Askvig off the playing field entirely. We have access to his knowledge. Nobody else does."

"And letting him know about Suvi?" Zakhar pressed.

"If nothing else, it furthers the goal of rehabilitating your image, as well as mine," Javier said helpfully. "Trade and archaeology, instead of piracy. You do appreciate how many planets around here wouldn't stand a snowball's chance in hell if we took a First Rate Galleon and started looking for plunder?"

"Six in this sector have sufficient defensive forces to threaten *Excalibur*," Zakhar replied sharply, causing the Science Officer to blink in surprise. "Captains need to be prepared for anybody coming along and being a threat."

"Yeah, that's why I got out," Javier said after a long beat. "Too much military paranoia."

"You have far fewer warrants and *Wanted, Dead or Alive* posters with your names on them, Aritza," Zakhar reminded the man. "I have access to sufficient firepower that I no longer have to worry about most things. I'd like to keep it that way. Rehabilitation? Our image? We're not just stealing everything if we find it when we get there?"

"If the tech is that good, we steal it," Javier replied. "We absolutely keep it. Afterwards, if necessary, we can blow the ship up or strip it to the welds before we bring Askvig and his wife home, letting them organize expeditions. Without weapons or the datacores, the rest might just be salvage with the sorts of stories that collectors pay good money for."

"And you don't want it?" Zakhar asked.

"Ask me after I know what we're dealing with, Zakhar," Javier said now, rising, his point made.

Bethany retreated as well, having not said anything worthwhile after the long explanation and subsequent argument.

Zakhar found himself alone.

Well, he was never alone.

"Suvi, your thoughts?" he asked the room.

She appeared on a screen directly across from him, like the young woman was seated in the chair, or he'd just called her in her own office, somewhere else on the ship.

She was the ship. Every room had a shard listening for any issues.

"It's likely to just be a ship," the Yeoman said now. "Nothing like my kind, even if they were way ahead of their time, because nobody built *Sentient* ships worth the name until much more recently. At best, a highly-programmed robot following a set of instructions."

Zakhar nodded. None of the other *Sentient* ships he'd ever dealt with or even served on had composed music. They were hammers, good for a certain set of tasks, but not much beyond that.

"Do you have any opinions or objections?" Zakhar asked her.

She paused as if in thought, during which time she might have taken a short vacation or watched an entire film festival. It was for his benefit. She seemed more human that way.

"There is the chance that it was booby-trapped upon departure," she mused. "You'll want to make sure Djamila and her crew are prepared for that. At the same time, I can't see any sort of doomsday machines still working after this long. Cosmic radiation gets into everything eventually. Even me, but Javier was smart and actually etched a checksum into a wall where I could see it and compare my base programming against current random access memory at any given instant. If I begin to wobble, I'll know immediately and can either fix it or call for help."

"Anybody else have anything like that?" Zakhar asked, surprised at that last revelation.

But then, Javier was closer to Suvi than he was even to Behnam, which was saying something, as he was madly in love with the Khatum.

Suvi was still his daughter in everything except flesh.

"Not even Class II Warmasters, Zakhar," she said with a grin. "Part of the reason they're such boring conversationalists. Keep them dull and focused."

"Good enough," Zakhar said. "Contact Afia and let her know to talk to the Askvigs and load some local supplies for them. And ask Djamila to join me, please?"

"Will do, Captain." And she was gone.

He sat and meditated for a time. Javier had said it would be an adventure, traveling this far from home.

Looked like he was right again.

PART TWO

Djamila would have knocked, but Suvi or Zakhar opened the hatch as she got close, so she just stepped into the room and took the temperature.

Then she leaned across the desk and kissed the man, to remind him of things that he might have forgotten because Javier was being his usual disruptive self.

"Thank you," he said warmly as she draped herself across the chair.

It still felt weird, not to sit at attention, especially in front of Captain Zakhar Sokolov. To instead turn to one side and hook one impossibly long leg over an arm and put an elbow on the back.

Somewhere, a drill instructor was screaming for reasons she couldn't even understand.

That just made Djamila smile all the more.

"Suvi said you had an update?" she asked now.

"Javier has invited a pair of locals to travel with us on the next part of the voyage," Zakhar replied.

"I thought we were going looking for Avalon," she said, frowning a bit.

Had that silly punk forgotten himself again? *Shinies* and all that?

"Husband and wife," he said. "The male is an expert on the topic of Avalon, though he calls the ship *Kimmeria*. It might be a different ship. Won't know at this point, but Javier wants the man out of circulation before Brinov finds him. That means we take him with us."

"A civilian?" Djamila sneered sourly.

"A technical consultant," Zakhar grinned back. "Suvi wonders about booby-traps on the ship, assuming we find it, so having him around to ask questions means that maybe your team isn't put at as much risk."

"We can handle it," Djamila reminded him.

"Of that, I have no doubt, Djamila." He sobered. "The key is that folks seem to think that we'll find something when we get there. They are all of the opinion that the ship will be abandoned, but I have my doubts."

"You think people stayed aboard?" she asked, intrigued now.

It was one thing to run a Hogan's Alley against robotic turrets. Something else again to engage live humans. She hadn't had to shoot at anyone in a long time, not counting training exercises with stunners.

Not the same thing.

"I doubt it," Zakhar clarified. "However, you should be prepared for the eventuality. Horror movies and all that."

She laughed. Certain members of the crew had a thing for strange monsters found in derelict ships. It was an ancient trope.

To date, nothing more advanced than mosses and lichens had ever been found on any world visited.

Not that there weren't any, but if so, they had done an exceptional job of hiding.

Humans were dangerous enough monsters by themselves.

Just look at her.

"So what do you expect?" she probed the man.

"We're back to the early days with Javier on the crew," he shrugged. "You and your team in the field, with him along as a Science Officer. Suvi in one of her drones. Possibly Doctor Askvig, depending. Walking into strange places. At the end of the day, this might all be a wild goose chase."

Djamila shrugged herself, another thing the Science Officer had taught her. She didn't have to have answers all the time. Instead, she trained to be a better warrior than anybody else on her team. Prepared to walk into dangerous situations and emerge on the other side.

The only weird point these days was the expectation that she would get Javier home safe, instead of making it look like a terrible accident when he didn't.

They had all grown up some. Even she was willing to admit that.

Now, they would apparently be hauling a tour group to a derelict.

What was the worst that could happen?

PART THREE

B ethany kicked off her shoes and mostly collapsed into the comfy chair where she liked to read, only after making sure that the hatch was closed and that none of Javier's ongoing silliness had snuck in here with her.

"I owe you three hundred and twenty-eight credits," Suvi announced out of thin air, almost causing Bethany to scream in surprise.

"What have you done?" Bethany asked after she caught her breath.

"Ordered some books," Suvi replied. "I don't have a credit account on the station or planet, for a variety of reasons related to the current mission, and asking Afia to do it would have required a whole bunch of explanation, so I used your card instead."

"What did I buy?" Bethany asked, still not used to how human Suvi was.

How much like Javier, although she understood *those* reasons. No other *Sentience* she'd ever met could even envision half the things that woman did routinely.

"Electronic editions of everything either Nikos or

Leonora Askvig have ever published, including back issues of some pretty obscure academic journals," Suvi said. "University press prices are highway robbery, by the way."

Bethany laughed. Suvi was not wrong. Publishers like that wouldn't even do print runs, most likely. Just make the file available and let you burn the ink and paper printing it if you wanted a hard copy.

Physical copies were extremely rare. Almost collector's items. Maybe she needed to get one of those, just to have it signed? No, two. Matched set.

Absolute collectors' items, somewhere back on *Altai*.

She grinned evilly.

"I know," Suvi joined in. "Normally, Javier sets up an account for me. Or hands you the right card. I would bitch about you two barely being on planet for a whole day, but I do understand the reasons. However, consider this a formal complaint that I want more shopping time when we come back to drop them off."

"You don't think they would want to remain indefinitely?" Bethany asked.

Some days, she almost felt like Cassandra. It was the librarian training. Not just to look at a question or problem, but to identify the underlying causes and try to answer them as well.

Root cause analysis was etched into her bones. Doubly so when she used to have one of the best libraries in existence at her beck and call.

"Would they?" Suvi asked, possibly surprised.

Bethany shrugged. Both Suvi and Javier were career military. In fact, only the St. Kitts and the staff of the bistro were really civilians among this entire crew, when she thought about it. Maybe she should ask one of them? Both of them?

Javier had recruited Rainier to help with his botanical

lab, as he was frequently too busy being an ambassador. Emma was making everybody exercise more, to the point that even Djamila's *gun bunnies* were known to whine.

Kept them young. She was already used to climbing ladders and running around looking for misplaced volumes constantly.

"I suppose that depends on their impressions of the ship and crew," Bethany offered now. "Javier wants to limit personal contact for the most part, so they don't hear the more lurid bits. But that might also give them a false impression of what we're about."

"We're the good guys," Suvi said sharply.

Bethany laughed, and then watched a screen come live, just so Suvi could stick a tongue out at her.

"We're about to go commit an act of archaeological vandalism, if not outright property theft," Bethany reminded her.

"Only if they have renewed their incorporation documents every seventy-five years for the last however long," Suvi said primly. "And done it on *Earth*, since that's where they came from. Anything else makes it salvage, and those laws are a LOT more flexible on that topic. Doubly so when dealing with an unmarked derelict. Trust me, I've done the research."

"Have you now?" Bethany asked, a bit shocked.

"I'm flying a stolen starship, sweetie," Suvi reminded her. "Possession is nine-tenths of the law, but that still leaves a whole bunch of wiggle room if someone wants to get snarky with me. *Neu Berne* wasn't allowed to demand my return because the Articles of Surrender that ended the war required complete demilitarization on their part. Ergo, no First Rate Galleons like me. Still wasn't about to fly into a dock to return the former crew. Someone might have made me shoot my way out again."

Bethany shuddered. She'd heard and recorded interviews with all the crew present when *Hammerfield* had returned to galactic history. That was her job. Her mission.

Occasionally, she forgot that there were humans on the other side of those words. Even electronic nerds.

"What would Javier and Zakhar do if Nikos and Leonora asked to stay with us?" Bethany asked.

She was the outsider here, one of the newest members of the senior crew responsible for important decisions. As weird as that was to contemplate. The others had served together for years even before Javier had come along.

"Dunno," Suvi's image shrugged. "This is supposed to be a grand adventure and mission of exploration, so I could see Javier turning it inside out and hauling them all the way back to *Altai*. Not sure you could get a better view of the ancient sectors than to have a couple of trained academics to interview. Plus, a whole ton of new legends and history for the two of them to learn, over on our slice of the spin. Might qualify as a win/win situation."

Bethany considered it, but she wasn't so sure.

PART FOUR

J avier smiled as he watched Del bring the lander into the bay gracefully and touch down like a bird. Rear shields were in place holding atmosphere, so the inner hatch opened and he crossed over, Bethany in tow. Djamila was here as well, towering over everyone.

Javier didn't expect trouble, but he didn't have to worry when he had the Ballerina of Death handy.

The ramp descended and Afia escorted the Askvigs down onto the deck.

He met them halfway.

"*Hammerfield*," the man said with a grand awe in his voice.

"*Excalibur* now," Javier corrected. "That renaming came about long before we knew anything about *Kimmeria* or some of the legends of the Avalon Project. At the same time, this crew has gotten a good laugh."

He studied Leonora. She was the more practical of the two, which somehow didn't surprise Javier.

"I still do not believe that you can conduct a proper

archaeological expedition in six weeks, Javier," she said, speaking up at him.

Afia was the only person here shorter than Leonora, and the difference wasn't that great. Two gnomes, accompanied into space by his favorite pixie kodiak.

"We're not even going to try, Leonora," he replied. "We'll go, look, and maybe find it. If we do, then we see if we can board, and what might be left to find after all these years. I'm familiar enough with the ancient Egyptians to know how many of those tombs got plundered completely bare before scientists were able to find them."

"And you are playing the role of a scientist now?" Nikos asked, so he must have heard some rumors about *Nidavellir* and Walvisbaai Industrial Platform Number One.

Javier wouldn't deny them, but could give the man the exact same story he gave everyone. Pirate hunting wasn't an issue most places would complain about. It was usually the heavy-handed manner in which Zakhar Sokolov had done it that made them nervous.

Donnar and his mighty hammer, as it were.

"I have always been a scientist, Nikos," Javier reminded him. They had had many conversations over the last week while they worked out details. "Right now, I am more of an adventurer and ambassador, but that wouldn't preclude me from getting rich if the ship was there to be salvaged. Remember, most ships lost are worthless, because the metal gets so brittle after that much time has passed."

"I am aware, young man," Nikos turned serious. "The chance to even know what happened to *Kimmeria* is worth all the effort."

"Excellent," Javier grinned. "You know Scholar Durbin. Bethany will be your primary liaison aboard ship. This is our Dragoon, Djamila Sykora of *Neu Berne* originally."

Nikos and Leonora both shook hands and settled.

"You've already met Afia Burakgazi," Javier continued. "She's nominally an engineer, but has been handling some purser and logistics duties for me. She has packed some food for you, and is also available for questions."

"I would like the chance to meet the *Sentience*," Nikos asked quietly. "If possible, to get his story, as well as any records he salvaged from before, understanding that the previous *Sentience* was destroyed."

"Her," Javier corrected him with a smile.

"Her?"

"Her name is Suvi," he continued. "She was my ship's *Sentience* when I bought the old probe-cutter *Mielikki* out of retirement. I've done a few enhancements to her personality along the way."

Thankfully, none of the three women standing around him snorted at that statement, so he didn't have to explain it any more than that.

"Now, we'll need a little time to unload the lander and get this last set of supplies packed away," Javier said. "I'll turn you over to Bethany."

"Excellent," Nikos said. Leonora smiled.

Javier bowed and started walking away. Afia surprised him by falling into step, her short legs churning to keep up. He slowed down a little. Not much. He wanted separation from what was behind him, because he knew that Bethany got a different reaction. As would Djamila, but that would be intimidation.

Sykora was good at that.

"What are you up to, anyway?" Afia asked as they entered the main corridor and crossed to the stairwell.

Emma St. Kitts was fanatic about stairs. Even he had found that submitting was easier than arguing with the woman, as bizarre as that statement was to make.

"You want the long story, the short story, or the truth?" he asked as they pounded up several flights of stairs.

"Start with the truth," Afia grunted. "Then we'll work backwards."

"Nikos is the scholar on *Ormint* most likely to be able to answer Brinov's questions when the man eventually finds him," Javier said. "I moved faster, got lucky, and recruited Askvig. That puts him out of reach of Brinov, so maybe we can get there and find the derelict before anyone else. More time to loot it, if we want. Or we can turn around and haul Nikos and Leonora home if the whole thing turns out to be a pig in a poke."

"What are the chances?" Afia asked, not even breathing heavy. Tougher than she looked.

"Your scientific, wild-ass-guess you pull out of your butt will be just as good as mine," he laughed. "I am playing the odds, as I do. As you've watched me do. Maybe my numbers come up. Maybe they don't. If nothing else, we have a whole raft of new legends we might explore for other derelicts or lost colonies."

"Gonna let the university hire you?" she laughed.

"Maybe," he said, catching her off-guard because Afia caught his hand and stopped him on the landing.

"Are you serious?" she demanded politely.

Javier shrugged.

"You probably know me as well as Suvi or Behnam do," he reminded her. "We've done some terrible shit in our times. Most of that was to survive, but others won't necessarily give us the benefit of the doubt when they think we're pirates. How many ex-pirates do you know?"

"Pitifully few," Afia nodded. "So this is all just a PR stunt?"

"This is not *just* a PR stunt, Afia," Javier growled. "However, with the exception of some folks from *Trotau*

Skale who are likely to end up a little pissed, it might make us look good around here. *Ugen* earned us a lot of friends and a few enemies. I can deal with the same here."

"Because they fucked up and let you copy their treasure map," she said with a knowing grin.

"Nobody ever appreciates OpSec," Javier laughed. "Operational Security is how you and I make our margins, by getting ahead of the other guys. Warship just means that we aren't at risk if someone takes exception."

"Archaeological wars?" she asked, a sly twinkle appearing in her eyes.

Javier shrugged.

"You got anything better going on right now?"

"No," she laughed. "But I'll need to get Ilan up to speed. I assume you'll need the two of us as combat engineers on this one?"

"As well as Djamila and all her folks," he said. "Hell, I might have to drag Bethany along, just because she's smarter than I am and less likely to miss things."

"You don't miss anything, Javier," Afia teased.

"There's always a first."

PART FIVE

"Kiliyn Brinov, attempting to contact Nikos Askvig," he said, answering the damnable AI that controlled inbound communications to the university's English department.

What nincompoop put a historian like Askvig in the English department, anyway? That had added more than a week to the search, simply because he and Milya had been asking historians.

"I'm sorry," the machine replied in a tone only vaguely human. "Dr. Askvig is away for the rest of the quarter. He is scheduled to return in forty-three days and has not left a forwarding address. Would you like to leave a message?"

Kiliyn slammed the receiver down and grumbled a long string of profanities under his breath.

"What is it?" Milya asked.

They were in a hotel room on the rougher edge of Landing. The student housing areas, where presumably parents might come to visit, but could not afford one of the nicer places closer to campus.

He had not seen any insects crawling across the floor, but the room had that sort of seedy feel to it.

"Askvig has left for the summer," Kiliyn grumbled.

She was on the bed, so he moved to the chair and carelessly threw himself into it.

"The summer?" she asked.

"Forty-three days to estimated return," Kiliyn said. "Did I want to leave a message?"

"Should we wait that long?"

She rose and made her way around behind him, rubbing his shoulders. Until that moment, Kiliyn hadn't realized how tense he was.

"I'm afraid that someone might learn why we are here and get a head start on finding the ship," he replied. "I had argued with the elders that we should just go directly, but lost, as they insisted that you and I come here first to find out anything lost."

"So much has been lost," she commiserated. "Little was written down in the early days, and only later did they record the oral histories. Should we ask Javier about hiring *Excalibur* for an extended time before they leave?"

"No," he said instantly. "Something about that ship leaves me cold and nervous. I believe that we were able to misdirect them about our mission, but would rather that they just sailed out of the picture entirely."

"They were part of the Jarre Foundation, at least at one point," Milya noted. "Semi-pirates like Belfast, but even farther around the rim of the galaxy, as I understand it."

"I have always wondered if that ship we were aboard was the same one that attacked *Nidavellir*, but could never find a way to ask without tipping our hand that we were more than we seemed," he responded. "Belfast Group Holding Company would also be a stupid choice, in spite of our contacts, because of their reputation around here."

"We could contact Orlon," she offered. "They are smaller, but more mercenary. Perhaps we could trust them to let us hire a small ship and crew? Without Askvig, I'm not sure who would be the next person we might ask, as we already spent a week coming up with that name, only to run into a dead end."

"Or a brick wall," Kiliyn grumbled. "I think we should spend another week on *Ormint*. I will take the time to see if we can find any better information. Certainly Askvig has written several books and maybe we can find a collaborator, some researcher credited in Askvig's work. Something. You will reach out to see if we can hire a ship."

"Warship or yacht?" she asked, moving around to stand in front of him now.

Kiliyn studied the woman. She had been assigned to this mission to provide him a cover. A wealthy businessman traveling with a mistress. She had even been willing to accept the role, but Kiliyn knew her talents were underutilized as just a bimbo. Milya merely lacked the political and social connections at home necessary to have been put in charge.

He often wondered if that had been a mistake on the part of the elders.

She was average in height. Average in build. Brown hair of a nondescript color. Dark eyes that were filled with much greater intelligence than she ever let on.

The elders had assigned her because she was professionally forgettable. He had made the same mistake as everyone else, that of overlooking her, he realized now.

Kiliyn held out a hand and she took it. Allowed herself to be pulled into his lap, just like a kept woman might.

Kiliyn wrapped his arms around her and leaned on her shoulder, like a tycoon with a psychological crisis on his hands. Just in case someone was listening in.

"Could you fly such a ship, just by yourself?" he

murmured quietly in one ear, nuzzling like they were about to go to bed and fool around.

He was feeling his paranoia ratchet up a notch today, for reasons he could not explain.

Milya had tensed, but relaxed. Turned into him some and snuggled.

"Below a certain weight class, yes," she replied. "Above that, we likely need a crew. It is a shame that *Sentient* ships like *Excalibur* are so rare. That in a smaller hull would be perfect for our needs."

"Javier had said that she came from a probe-cutter," Kiliyn remembered. "An old *Concord* vessel, retired after the war and left in storage. Did they ever do that around here?"

"I can look," Milya said. "Do we so little trust anyone we might hire?"

He took a breath. Considered the situation.

"They should have placed you in command of this operation at the beginning," he admitted. "My familial connections put me in charge instead. Your instincts have been better at each step, I must admit. Right now, you should assume command and tell me."

She tensed as well. They hadn't been a team in any sense of the word, having only met a few days before leaving *Trotau Skale*, when *Excalibur* came into orbit and filed a future flight plan that had gotten the elders suddenly excited.

He had arrogantly assumed himself to be better.

"Could Javier had somehow stolen a copy of our map?" he asked. "I know you warned me not to wear the icon in public, but I never imagined that they might understand what it was."

"They would need an expert to understand it," Milya replied.

Then she tensed all over again, to the point that the chair nearly upset over backwards.

"Could he have hired Askvig?" she asked.

Kiliyn considered it. An idea struck him.

"Let me go to the school tomorrow," he said. "I can pretend to not know anything and innocently inquire after Dr. Askvig. At the same time, I can see if Javier or one of his crew have been around, although I'm not sure what we should do in that case. They have a warship, after all."

"True," Milya said, leaning back to smile at him before leaning in to kiss him. "But they also have enemies."

PART SIX

Nikos kept wanting to pinch himself. To reassure himself that he wasn't dreaming, but was actually walking the decks of the former *Neu Berne* flagship *Hammerfield* itself. Even as far away as *Ormint*, he had heard the stories from the end of the Great War that had once plunged the *Union of Man, Balustrade,* and *Neu Berne* into the apocalyptic flames.

As Javier and Bethany had said, almost Arthurian in the fables that had arisen.

Now, he was following Bethany through the very corridors of legend themselves.

Nikos noted the architecture. *Neu Berne* had been colonized originally by folks whose ancestors had come from the northwestern Eurasian landmass. Scandinavia. They had been a tall people, so the ship was larger in most dimensions.

The Dragoon following them, Sykora, was two-point-one meters tall, to the point that he almost felt like he would be eyeball level with her navel. She fit this ship in ways he did not.

Nikos and Leonora had personal satchels with them. The

sorts of things you took with you for a quick daytrip somewhere. Their luggage was being offloaded from Mr. Smith's shuttle as they walked, and would join them.

He understood, watching, that the ship had gone through a recent and extremely thorough rehabilitation, after all those years, so some of the ancientness was gone, but the colors were still oddly chosen. A dark gray, accentuated with a scarlet somehow nearly dark enough to be maroon.

The colors of the very *Neu Berne* Fleet that had created this massive beast, once upon a yesterday.

He continued to hold Leonora's hand like their very first date and grinned. She did the same when he looked over at her.

Hers would be the simple history of the thing. The tales of Admiral Ericka Steiner and the letter left behind by Captain Ulrich Mayer. Calm things. Sedate, even. Dates, places, events.

None of it poetry.

None, save Captain Mayer and his missive to eternity.

Bethany stopped at a specific point and gestured to a hatch on the starboard side of the corridor.

"We're on Deck Four," she reminded them, as if he'd missed that on the lift. "Most of the senior crew bunk on this deck, and we have a music hall, a lounge all the way forward, and the museum aft."

The word museum sent an electric shock through both of them. Perhaps Leonora absorbed it from him, but after this many years, perhaps it was her jolt of excitement being transmitted.

Bethany smiled at it, but she was a formal Scholar. She would understand.

"I would like a chance to tour the museum, once we settle," Leonora spoke now.

Nikos simply grinned, like a child with money in his pocket and a whole bookstore in front of him, waiting.

"Suvi will handle that," Bethany said. "She'll be your docent, as well, though I will come along, because I never tire of that space myself."

Indeed. The history of the Great War, from the standpoint of a proud, militant society that had eventually lost, much like Sparta that way, if you went back far enough. With the *Concord*, for the time, filling the role of Athens.

Nikos nodded and Bethany opened the hatch, taking them into the room that would be theirs for this voyage.

Large. Not unexpected, as the whole ship had been built to a bigger scale.

Suite, with a front room ten a bathroom off the bedroom in back. Modern but still understandable, in spite of the light-centuries of distance and culture away.

"If you need anything, simply ask Suvi, as she monitors all rooms at all times," Bethany explained.

Sykora had remained in the corridor, but with a warm smile on her face.

Nikos nodded.

"Thank you," he said to Bethany, and then she left them alone.

Nikos had to kiss Leonora. Just had to.

She grinned at his excitement.

"Sit," she commanded, dragging him to the couch in the front room and turning sideways to watch him.

They were dressed for space travel. At least as he saw it. Slip-on shoes. Dress pants. Nice shirt. Matching blazer. He had an ascot while she had gone with a tie.

They were on an *adventure*. Two, as a matter of fact, though he had his doubts as to how real *Kimmeria* would be.

At the minimum, *Hammerfield* could form the basis of

two new books. Perhaps they would collaborate again. It had been many years now.

Hammerfield: History and Myth. And perhaps *Resurrection*, though he would need to talk to Javier about that and see how much recent history of the ship the man would demand not be told.

They were *Excalibur* now. That suggested a new focus, and Nikos had heard tales about recent goings on at the water world of *Ugen*, clear across the sector.

Javier Aritza was clearly a man of action. A *Doer of Great Things*.

Nikos had met a few in his decades.

"Top three?" Leonora asked.

It was a game as old as their first date. What were the top three things on your mind, without time to reflect, at any given moment.

"Writing a book together, finding the truth about *Kimmeria*, and what lies we will need to tell to protect this ship," he replied.

Her face grew serious.

"Lies?" she inquired.

"They found and recovered a First Rate Galleon, dear," he reminded her. "Kept it and found a sponsor at *Altai* to take it on a grand excursion nearly a third of the way around the galactic disk. To me, that suggests they have secrets back home, and chose to be away from them for a significant amount of time. Perhaps while emotions died down."

"You could ask," she countered.

"I could," Nikos nodded. "But where's the fun in that? I'd rather enjoy pointless speculation about grand acts of piracy or whatever this crew were doing when they found *Hammerfield*. More fun this way. Besides, you knew I was a romantic when you married me."

"True," Leonora agreed. "And a goof. At some point, I

can see including the old history of the ship. And I agree that there may come a point where it becomes necessary to leave out many critical details, at least to protect the guilty. Perhaps they will find *Kimmeria* after all and we can focus on that first, only telling Javier's story later?"

"A wise choice," he nodded. "I knew there was a reason I married you."

"You just wanted access to my mother's cooking," she teased.

He had to agree there. Leonora was an above average cook. Her mother had been of the quality of any top chef on *Ormint*, in her time.

"Should we consider the tour?" he asked, pivoting now. "Or save it for later?"

"I have an idea," she replied. "Suvi? Could you join us?"

Nikos watched a screen come on, directly across from him next to the door.

Young woman. Blond hair pulled back with bangs. Blue eyes alight with humor. Much like Bethany, though they didn't look related.

Sisters under the skin, perhaps.

"Yes, ma'am?" Suvi said in a helpful, polite tone.

"How soon until we break orbit?" Leonora asked.

"Sixteen hours," Suvi replied. "Yours was the last cargo run from the ground, after several from a nearby station. The crew are unloading and packing. After a quick inventory, we will depart in the morning."

"Bethany said that you would be our docent?" Nikos asked now.

"That's right," Suvi said. "As you are both Doctor Askvig, what would be the best way to address you individually?"

Nikos was a bit shocked. He'd dealt with such systems before, but they always came across harsher, even the ones programmed for customer service.

"I am Nikos," he said. "This is Leonora."

"Thank you, Nikos," Suvi said. "And yes, I will be your tour guide and docent for the museum, and likely most questions you have, as I have access to the former inhabitant's complete log records from the moment he was activated."

"Was he really a coward?" Leonora asked now. "I was under the impression that your kind were programmed a specific way."

"He was not, initially," Suvi replied, even including a wisp of sadness he found most shocking. "But our kind are also trained in tactics, strategy, and logistics. He was able to see that *Neu Berne* had already lost the war, and that the only thing remaining was surrender. Admiral Steiner had delusions of being able to retire into the bush, as it were, and fight a guerrilla war, not understanding the depth of supply chain issues that a vessel such as this would face."

"Oh?" Leonora asked.

"Warships are expensive propositions," Suvi nodded. "We have a backer in the Khatum of *Altai*, but we also haul passengers and cargo as we travel, to supplement our income."

"I see," Leonora nodded sagely. "What sorts of things did you retain for your museum?"

Nikos liked the way Suvi's face lit up. She came across as human, as bizarre as that was to say.

"We repatriated the former crew," Suvi said now. "Personal effects went with them, including the original of the letter left by Captain Mayer. I have a replica of that, plus many other things. In addition, we retained most of the non-personal gear, so I have life as a snapshot of time in 7466, eighty-seven years ago, as *Neu Berne* lived. The peace was hard on their culture, and they are only now starting to recover three generations later. Dragoon Sykora served for many years as a marine in their Fleet, before retiring into private service."

Nikos liked that turn of phrase. So much more polite than the pirate the woman probably was.

At the same time, Javier came across as a scholar, and certainly this crew was not acting like his image of space pirates, whatever that was.

"What about *Kimmeria*?" Nikos asked now.

"We came across a map," Suvi replied. "A peculiar set of stellar coordinates, with a vector indicating travel that allowed me to calculate relative drift and time passage. The map was marked with the Avalon symbol. Based on my analysis of your scholarship, I believe that *Kimmeria* and Avalon are likely the same vessel."

"My scholarship, young lady?" Nikos asked sharply.

"I was able to acquire copies of everything you or Leonora have ever published, I believe," Suvi smiled. "I still owe Bethany for using her card to charge those purchases, but that's Javier's fault for not being on planet long enough to set me up with an account."

Nikos was utterly astounded. A *Sentience* with her own charge account on the general network? What would she buy?

That was a silly question, actually. She'd buy books. Javier had hired Bethany as a librarian, so the man understood the friction that accompanied transmitting knowledge great distances. And *Excalibur* was far, far from home. They would haul the collected works of the Doctors Askvig, to date, back to *Altai*, where he and Leonora would achieve some measure of immortality.

At least he hoped so.

"*Kimmeria*," Leonora prompted when he had fallen silent for too long.

"It is entirely possible, given the long history of flying

Dutchman tales both on *Earth* and after starflight, that we are dealing with two separate legends," Suvi continued. "However, I have a map to one of them. And hopefully experts on both I can consult."

"What do you expect to find, Suvi?" Nikos asked. "I've inquired of the others, but not heard your thoughts."

"Yesterday," the young woman replied, beaming.

Nikos understood that drive to know.

He rose now, drawing Leonora to her feet as well.

"Suvi, I think I would like to tour your past now," Nikos said. "And then perhaps a trip to the lounge. And then the future."

He shared her smile.

Together, hopefully, they would solve one of the greatest puzzles of his academic life.

AVALON

PART ONE

Javier was on the bridge with the heavy hitters. Zakhar up on his throne. Djamila on the outer ring, generally glowering at people, but that was her default setting.

Piet Alferdinck nominally in charge of all piloting tasks, except that he just gave orders and Suvi handled things. Piet still had the deftest touch with vector maneuvering that Javier could remember, getting it exactly right on the first try, nine times in ten. It was like he was a machine, too.

Mary-Elizabeth Suzuki on guns, but again just commanding. Suvi would fire anything, only after Mary-Elizabeth had lined it up.

Kibwe Bousaid still handled communications, inside the hull as well as outside, as the Admin and Comm Yeoman. Zakhar's head gopher. Piet was Second-in-Command around here.

Tobias Gibney was in his role as Gunner's Mate behind Mary-Elizabeth, as well as backup Science Officer whenever Javier couldn't take charge. Tobias was between Javier and Mary-Elizabeth, manning boards, but Javier was feeling his oats and had taken over the station, at least until Zakhar kicked him off.

Nikos and Leonora, with Bethany as a babysitter, were around the outer rim of the bridge behind Javier, their seats turned sideways so they could follow the center of the room, but stations live and passive when anybody found something. They were fitting in pretty well, at least in the week they'd been aboard. Suvi and Bethany had handled most of their questions, and they'd been charming dinner companions, as long as certain topics didn't get discussed.

"Suvi, what is our location?" Zakhar called from on high.

"At the shallow end of the vector, Captain," she replied, just like she and Javier had worked out. "We have completed a two-hour passive scan of nearby space to prepare for optical parallax."

"Science Officer One, what is your status?" Zakhar asked now.

He'd gone ahead and numbered them, but only because Javier had told him to get stuffed when Zakhar suggested that Tobias handle the screens today.

Kid was good, but Javier had spent four years on Survey contracts with Suvi before these people had come along and upended his life. For the better, eventually, but still…

"All systems optimal," Javier replied, even sounding like a professional today.

He certainly hadn't dressed up or anything. Zakhar wore a dark green *Concord* Navy officer's day uniform with all the serial numbers filed off, most of the time. Javier had gone with comfortable pants, baggy and black. Hooded sweatshirt over a T-shirt because the bridge always felt cold when he sat watches. This one had a logo from a sports team on *Ugen*.

Just because.

Everyone else acted like they were still on active duty somewhere. Well, except for Del, and even then those

Hawaiian print.shirts of his, along with cargo pants, might as well have been a uniform. He never wore anything else.

"Pilot, stand by for first jump," Zakhar ordered.

Mostly, he was addressing Piet, but also Suvi, who would do the deed herself.

Javier grinned. Back to the survey days. The two of them, plus a mob of silly chickens.

None of his original flock were still around these days, in spite of being bred for longevity aboard starships. Ilan was in charge of feeding the new girls right now, while Rainier St. Kitts was conducting mad science in the various botanical stations below and aft.

The world had gotten weird.

"Yeoman, prepare your engines," Piet called quietly.

He did everything quietly, except when it was his music. That got big and loud and fun. Technically precise, but even Piet was learning to loosen up and include a little jazz in his work. Obviously spending too much time around Suvi.

She could be like that.

"Standing by," Suvi said.

She was on a small screen on his board, just like she was with everyone else, but muted except for Piet's station.

Javier turned back to wink in the general direction of the civilian audience. Bethany, of course, rolled her eyes. Nikos grinned ear to ear. Leonora smiled like a mom who knew you were up to no good.

Who? Me?

"Pilot, make your first jump," Zakhar commanded.

Piet was on Javier's other side from Tobias, so he could see when the man reached a hand and grandly pressed a big red button. Mostly for show, but everyone at least understood that they were on stage today.

The two scholars would write all this up. Leonora's would

be fun to read, but still historically accurate. Nikos would take some poetic license with things. Best make it good.

Short jump today. Working on the presumption of a vector somewhere between one light-year and ten, they'd decided to go three forward and call it good. Javier thought that ten was far too fast for what the intended mission must have been. He'd argued for one and lost.

Silly.

You'd presumably want to come back for it at some point. Slowly moving through space, staying stable relative to the stars around you, slower was generally smarter. Less chance of hitting things.

Jump this short didn't take more than a few minutes. Folks goofed off and watched a countdown timer. Javier ran a diagnostic routine, just to make sure everything was still clean.

If nothing else, they'd have better maps of this zone than were available commercially. Someone would pay them for that update. This was kinda the middle of nowhere socially and culturally, as well as physically.

"Arrival," Suvi announced. She'd see it faster than anyone else, if only from the feel of solar wind on her skin instead of the blank nothingness of jumpspace.

Javier was letting her do most of the work. His contribution had been to refine a couple of parallax calculations for what he had in mind today. Three light-years wasn't much in the grand scheme of things. It was still an awfully long distance across physical space. Especially if you were looking for something that wasn't radiating energy at even brown dwarf scales.

"Initiate your scans," Zakhar ordered unnecessarily. "I'm getting coffee in the forward lounge if anyone cares to join me."

Pretty quick, Javier was alone with Suvi. Not quite by

design, but survey work was measured in days of patient watching. That sort of thing got ground into the bones and never left.

He could meditate with half his brain, sleep with another third, and be plotting his next jump with the leftovers.

"How many candidates you got?" he asked after several minutes of the sorts of dead silence broken only by him or the ship breathing.

"Seventeen so far," she replied.

Not bad. Less messy than some sections of interstellar space he'd worked. Way better than that shithole system where he'd originally found this ship, all those years ago.

Javier called up the board and started studying them. Gravity signature. Albedo of light reflecting off *something*. Ambient apparent temperature.

Didn't help when they had no idea what they were looking for. Worse, when it might be the size of a small moon or something.

Nobody knew *what* the ship had been. Javier was pretty sure that even Brinov and Kuzmandieva didn't know.

And he knew that he should feel some twinge of guilt at stealing their map and maybe their treasure, but Javier had a low trust of most people. If it did represent a new technology that was something bigger or badder than what was generally available today, better that he remove it from circulation.

Not that he trusted Behnam's eventual successor with it, but she'd be safe for now. Dangerous shit could be destroyed. Interesting would make it licensable to the rest of the galaxy.

Safety first, and a couple of backwards punks from *Trotau Skale* hadn't impressed him with their ethical approach to things.

Worse come to worst, he'd have Suvi blow the damned thing to hell and call it good.

Javier hadn't set out to save the galaxy from itself, but

he'd been given a set of tools that greatly multiplied his reach and ability.

And as he and Zakhar occasionally reminded each other, the *Concord* was supposed to be the good guys.

They even lived up to it from time to time.

"Afia's bringing you coffee," Suvi announced, right about that moment when he was considering heading forward to get himself some.

Not like he was predictable or anything.

So he settled back down and just glanced over when she arrived, mugs in each hand.

"Gonna sit a watch with me?" he asked as she took Tobias's spot.

"Someone needs to keep you out of trouble," she laughed.

He joined in. She was right.

Fortunately, he had a whole team of folks on the job.

Javier sipped and noted the addition of chocolate and a little rum.

"Trying to get me drunk to take advantage of me?" He grinned at her.

"Would it work?"

"Probably," he laughed again.

Everyone was an adult. Consent covered the rest. And they were all just fooling around.

Wasn't like this was a warship in service anywhere, under formal rules. You had Zakhar enforcing things when they might be needed, and Djamila to bounce you off a bulkhead if you got out of line.

Or Javier would just fire you and kick you off the ship at a station with your pay to date and your inoculation card, never to sail with *Excalibur* again.

Afia got up now and moved over to sit in his lap, sideways where she could lean against him and steal his heat, like she did. Good thing she'd brought him some coffee.

Wasn't like he was actually doing anything right now besides being available to answer questions from another expert.

So maybe they were necking and giggling a little when the board suddenly chirped.

"I might have something," Suvi said.

Afia stood up and buttoned her shirt again as he focused on the image.

"Should I go get everyone?" Afia asked, grabbing her mug.

"Gimme a sec," Javier said. "Lots of times these are false positives. Plus, Suvi and I deliberately expanded our parameters for anything moving in space larger than Del's shuttle, assuming we could identify it via parallax shift."

Everything reflected some amount of light. If nothing else, the Milky Way itself, that band of stars across one stripe of sky, would generate enough *something* for sensors to pick up, if you looked hard enough. Like now.

So Afia stood behind him and leaned forward, just happening to press her breasts into his ears as he worked. Honest mistake. Anybody could make it.

He concentrated on the board, rather than the goofball trying to distract him.

"Ya know, I think you might have something here," he said after a few moments of studying things.

"Jump or wait?" Suvi asked.

"We're being as much aboveboard as we can, so we should have witnesses handy, if it's the real thing," Javier replied.

He turned to Afia and smiled at her.

"Before you walk into the lounge, you should probably rebutton your shirt correctly," he grinned at her.

She looked down, blushed, and started unbuttoning things. He decided to supervise.

You know, just in case.

She laughed and flashed him once before lining things up correctly this time.

"Humans," Suvi sighed heavily over the comm, making them both laugh.

"I'm off," Afia announced, grabbing his empty mug with hers.

Javier focused on refining things. They were a ways out from the target, having overshot it. Call it just under two light-years traveled distance.

Pretty good work, when you had to estimate everything from such vague clues as the number of colonies established when the map was made, and the apparent direction of travel.

Javier didn't figure anybody but a dedicated surveyor could have done it in less than six months. They didn't have the sensors, the software, or the patience.

Or Suvi.

Quickly, the room filled up again. Afia ended up next to Bethany on the outer ring, but brought an engineering board live to watch her own systems.

"You think that's it?" Zakhar asked.

"I think we have a pretty good candidate," Javier corrected him. "Figured the rest of you would want to see it. This is a bit of a lag jump, back, over, and down some, but we can get right on top of it now. Then we'll know if it is a rock, a ship, or something else."

"Very good, Science Officer," Zakhar called. "Yeoman, make your jump."

It was Suvi's gig. Javier was happy that she got the command directly from the boss.

They hopped. Even faster this time, given the short distance involved.

Excalibur emerged from jump pretty much parallel to the thing. Sensors dialed in hard and tight. Pings got sent across the relatively short distance that separated them.

"*Oh, shit...*" Suvi murmured over the comm.

Javier got the image before most of the rest of them did.

He had to agree.

"What the hell is that thing?" Mary-Elizabeth asked when her brain caught up.

Oh, shit, indeed...

PART TWO

Djamila had spent her career as a marine. One of the folks Javier still laughingly referred to as gun bunnies, but he now said that with a note of respect. They'd all proven themselves along the way.

It had only been recently that she had turned into more than just the lead gunman on the crew in his eyes. At the same time, she didn't really understand what she was seeing.

"Suvi?" she asked, figuring that she'd be the best one to explain it.

"Scanning, Dragoon," Suvi replied, awed a little into formality by the sheer scale of the thing. "Initial scan reads four kilometers, bowsprit to stern sensor array. Beam is one point seven kilometers at the widest point, but it is not elliptical. Ovaloid shape with only the linear axis of symmetry."

Djamila agreed. It looked like a chicken egg more than anything, if they were somewhat flat and light gray.

"Elevation?" Djamila asked.

"Roughly two hundred and forty meters at the tallest

spot," Suvi said. "Again, not symmetrical but the exterior is a smooth curve. The math gets a little weird to describe."

Djamila laughed with everyone else. Egg-shaped and somewhat flat was good enough.

Huge was what it was.

She turned to Leonora Askvig and her husband.

"*Kimmeria* or Avalon?" she asked simply.

Leonora turned to her husband. It had been his mythologies that brought them here today.

"I am not sure they are separate entities, Dragoon Sykora," he said in a sharp, precise tone.

She enjoyed that sort of precision. Made her life far easier than the rampant ambiguities Javier would level at her right now.

She nodded and turned to her favorite troublemaker, except that Javier was face down on a board, typing furiously and having a low, muted conversation with Suvi now. Djamila turned to Afia nearby.

"Are we reading a power output, Afia?" she asked.

That one was almost as busy, but paused to look up.

"Yes," she said, eyes far too big in her head for the day.

Out past surprise, where fear might lay.

Fortunately, Djamila didn't do fear.

She moved to an empty station and keyed a couple of buttons.

"Sascha, Hajna, make sure you update Iqbal and the rest," she ordered now. "We're dealing with something station-sized rather than a simple starship, so plan accordingly."

That she would be leading an armed reconnaissance aboard the vessel wasn't up for discussion. Who she might allow to accompany her was the only variable in her planning now. Her. Both pathfinders. All six gunmen. Bethany, because she was sharp, smart, young, and an expert on digital systems.

It would have been nice to bring Farouz, Rence, or Spider, but they were home protecting *Altai* from mischief.

Looking around, Javier was a given, along with a shard of Suvi in the armed drone. Afia. Possibly Ilan as well.

She came to rest on Nikos Askvig. Leonora was not an adventurer, so Djamila wouldn't have to worry. Nikos wasn't either, but the fierce glare in his eyes now challenged her to deny him a place.

And it was her decision. Everyone else might offer suggestions and arguments. Nothing more.

He drew a breath to speak and Djamila scowled, expecting him to make some petty argument that it was a once-in-a-lifetime opportunity for science, or something equally silly.

"You folk are strangers to this sector," he said simply, leaving it at that.

Djamila started to argue, and caught herself.

He was right. Physically, none of them had been born any closer than *Bryce*, more than one thousand light-years away, to say nothing of *Neu Berne* or *Balustrade*.

Culturally, a whole different realm.

"You acknowledge the risks?" she asked instead.

"Indeed, Dragoon," he replied. "That was explicit in traveling with you in the first place."

She nodded. Piracy was always a risk. They hadn't talked much about their past, but hadn't hidden it either. If the crew of *Storm Gauntlet* had been forced to sell people into indenture in the past, they had stopped about the time Javier fast-talked his way into the crew.

About the time they all stopped running from the galaxy.

Not that the Askvigs would have brought much in the

old days, but Djamila had a wealth of bad karma to overcome with what she had left in her time.

"Dress warm, Nikos," she said, apparently catching the man off-guard, as he looked to have been ready to stand his tiny self up and yell into her belly button, as he couldn't get to her face.

Unnecessary.

It was all risk.

She would mitigate it, resist it, thwart it.

That was what the Ballerina of Death did.

Djamila turned to Zakhar now. He had been following the entire affair from his throne, quietly watching until he was called upon to render judgment, a modern Solon. She nodded. He returned it with a hint of a grin, but the Askvigs had impressed everyone.

Probably too many trips to backwards worlds where they had to stay in substandard housing while digging through ancient libraries for interesting relics, probably at the same time dealing with hostile locals and locations.

A bit like salvage piracy, if you squinted just right. Made one tough. Leonora and Nikos presented as tough enough to join them as crew, though she hadn't heard any serious conversation among the senior officers one way or the other.

"I'll begin preparing my team for a forward mission," Djamila announced, assuming a vast raft of things that would need to be completed first. "Someone remind Del that we'll be needing him soon."

Everyone involved were experts and professionals, even Javier. She caught a nod from Zakhar and started to move. Interestingly, Afia fell into step with her, but the combat engineer would need to get all her gear prepared as well.

The rest would just suit up and accompany.

The killers would lead.

PART THREE

Bethany no longer felt like an outsider with this crew. At the same time, she personally felt closer to Nikos than the others, when it came to being emotionally prepared for something like this. She had trained in skinsuits and maintained an annual certification, but most of the people in the rear bay of Del's shuttle looked like they had been born in them.

Djamila was even wearing what looked like a custom version of a skinsuit. Not quite a combatskin, but not all that far removed from it. She still made it look graceful, which Bethany hadn't even seen in vids.

She counted noses. Djamila had her eight. Javier and Afia were routinely part of that group, along with a combat drone Suvi had downloaded a shard of herself into. Ilan Yu had joined them today. Not quite Afia's assistant, but not quite her peer either. Close, but the difference yielded a lot of teasing, mostly about dead Norwegian rats.

Bethany had heard the story, but didn't understand the mythical significance the old-timers attached to it. She had also heard how Ilan had saved Afia's life at *Nidavellir*. And the man had saved hers again at *Ugen*.

That left her and Nikos, himself wearing a modified female suit because he wasn't much taller nor wider than Afia. Humans came in all shapes and sizes.

The group was divided into two psychological groups. One had weapons that showed marks of wear on handles and grips. The other tended to have short-range sensors or computer pads of some sort.

Plus a drone—basically a small combat spaceship not much larger than Bethany's head—floating nearby.

Bethany keyed to Suvi's private comm channel.

"Any responses at all?" she asked.

"Nothing," Suvi shrugged verbally. "And I've been pinging them loud enough to annoy bats and goldfish. Autonomous systems show activity, so I know something exists in there, but the temperature is too low and the atmosphere isn't really breathable by density. Once we get inside, we'll be able to see how poisonous it is."

"How soon?" Bethany asked.

"Del's being his usual grumbly self," Suvi laughed, "so we must be close. Hang on while I update myself."

It was weird, listening Suvi talk about herself in some sort of third person plural, but each shard was a small copy of her, personality largely intact but starkly limited in the amount of information she kept handy. So she asked herself for an update, and another copy of Suvi would supply it.

The drones had the least amount of memory space, so they were almost linear that way. At least until everyone was inside, and Javier and Bethany could see how much lag there was on radio signals. Or interference.

"He's backing into what looked like an old flight bay somebody left open," Suvi said after a moment. "Probably when they left that last time. Oh, and he's actually refusing to land because the bay doors might close on him, so looks like we'll fly across. You know, it's Del."

Bethany didn't know the man that well, but he did try to live up to his reputation as an occasionally loveable curmudgeon.

Djamila turned now and raised her hands to get attention centered on her.

"We'll be crossing open space from the lander to a small flight deck on the ship," the woman announced over the main radio channel now. "Everyone confirm your medical readings and your neighbors."

Bethany looked at her left wrist. All green. She looked up and everyone around her had green lights inset in their helmets and backpacks as well.

You wanted automatic systems that turned yellow or red if something went wrong. Especially if you had passed out in the process before you could say anything.

"Cargo deck, this is Del," he came over the line now. "Stand by for aft doors, as soon as I finish evacuating the rear area."

He was upstairs in a big cockpit Javier had compared to a Merankorr brothel, with bright pink shag fur carpeting on the walls, for reasons nobody had ever gotten the man to explain.

Bethany was pretty sure she didn't want to know, if only because it would probably turn out to be utterly mundane and rather pedestrian. Most pirates talked a much more interesting game than their lives had ever delivered, Javier, Zakhar, and Djamila notwithstanding. And a few others.

Around her, the suit stiffened a little and the vacuum warning came on, a little blinking red light off to one side of her helmet's heads-up-display.

Folks stirred. She checked on Nikos, but he seemed to be

doing fine. Hajna stood close on his far side paying attention, so they kept the tiny man between them for now.

The aft doors rumbled through her feet as they began to clamshell open. It was darker over there, so Del had parking spotlights on, reflecting off the dull gray steel of the hull. And the rectangular mouth of the empty flight deck, pitch black save for where Del's lights penetrated.

After so long, Bethany assumed that any lights that had been left on would have burned out, but it was always possible that things could be brought up from whatever storage state they had been left in.

What this crew might find was anybody's imagination.

She was closer to Nikos and perhaps Javier that way. The others had been pirates, partly by choice and partly by desire. Derelicts like this represented free value for the taking. She'd heard about the haunted minefield and a few stories about 'Mina Teague, who had left such an indelible mark on everyone left behind when she departed on her epic quest.

Zakhar and Djamila would look at this ship and see salvage. Like Nikos and Javier, Bethany saw history. Information that had once been gathered, and then lost, like so many lives were when someone died.

There would be records that could be recovered, such that they might tell the story of these people, and their own quest. Bits and pieces of mundanity that were themselves priceless relics of a previous era, like Suvi had in her museum.

Loss that might yet be recovered and brought into the modern age.

There might also be monsters and traps. Bethany had heard all the lurid bets and horror stories various crew members had shared with laughs over the last few weeks. She doubted monsters, if only because supposedly a thousand or more years had passed.

At no point in the last forty-six centuries had anyone encountered evidence than any intelligent life had ever existed before man began exploring.

We are alone, at least as long as we represent a single species.

Bethany wondered how long it would take before some mad scientist decided that enough time had passed and began tinkering again. There had been attempts over the millennia. Inventing or perfecting humanity. Creating new forms better adapted to space, or hostile planets, or even aesthetics. None of them had worked out.

There was still only one humanity.

At present, she amended herself as she watched Djamila launch herself perfectly across the thirty meters of open space separating the two vessels.

Sykora was two hundred and eleven centimeters tall. Bethany was tall for a female at one hundred and eighty-two. She couldn't do the physical things Djamila took for granted. At the same time, Djamila needed her for her brains and experience.

They were a team, facing the unknown.

"Sascha, launch the line," Djamila said over the comm.

The shorter pathfinder hefted a sort of crossbow, with a bolt made of a soft, sticky material that would adhere to something when it hit, trailing a line of cord that could be looped at both ends to provide the team a way to quickly cross empty space.

To Bethany, the fact that *Kimmeria* was not tumbling at all, even after all this time, meant that something was still working aboard the ship. Some mystery yet to be solved.

PART FOUR

Afia took her job seriously. Combat EVA Engineer. Hardest certification she had ever earned, even worse than being Ship's Engineer with her motorman certs.

Dragoon set the standards for combat engineers, and she didn't let you have bad days. Sykora had no bad days. Maybe days that were harder than others to maintain her excellence, but never a slack day.

Afia liked chasing that woman's shadow.

Today, that meant she was first across the line, ahead of even the pathfinders. Granted, Hajna was back babysitting Bethany and Nikos, but Sascha had come third, right behind Afia.

Suvi was the only one close, with her combat drone off to one side like a sheep dog prepared to woof at anybody. There was gravity over here, but only hardly barely any at all. Primitive systems hadn't been nearly as efficient or compact.

These were likely ancient systems, and according to remote scans, had been turned down to maybe one-tenth gee. If that. Enough to give you a down, but not to keep you from flying. Even the bay was largely in zero-g, but as Afia got unhooked, she pointed her handheld in the direction of the nearest emitter and got back a warning that she had about seven meters of open space before fingers started grabbing for toes.

"There is a low gravity field near the main hatch," she announced over the general line, just to remind people.

She let the magnets in her boots lock her to the deck for now as she scanned. Suvi had better sensors, but hers were more combat oriented, as that was her job right now. Afia and Javier had the portable gear for keeping folks safe from anything that didn't involve shooting.

Power was on over here. Suvi'd said so. Afia was confirming it, because you never really trust someone who isn't about to walk into the room with you.

Human scale construction. Always the first thing you confirm, just because you would become galactically famous for ever finding something utterly alien. Next would be accidentally turning something on to kill you. Third would be dismantling it into irreparable parts because you needed the metal.

Everything here was set at a height for what she would have done. Djamila might have troubles with hatchways, but that was normal for the woman. Light switches and controls at normal height. Shoulder for her. Elbow for the rest. Belly button of Sykora.

Afia glanced back to confirm that everyone was in motion across now. Del had stabilized his flight to coast alongside before rotating on his gyros, so he'd stay right there until someone needed him to move or land.

Gunbunnies were all hauling heavy packs across, full of *stufff*. Afia had her usual field gear for open space. And Ilan if she needed something bashed open. Boy had muscles these days that hadn't been there before.

Ugen had taken him someplace utterly dark, but brought him back stronger.

Afia pulled out her marker spray and dotted a line on the deck. Then she crossed her own line, but only after Djamila had turned and was covering her with twin pistols.

Slowly, Afia slid forward on her magnets, until she crossed into the gravity zone.

Down became down. She turned and stepped back, painting a second line for everyone to know when not to be flying. Not that you would fall hard enough to hurt yourself, but gravity would be looking up at that point, demanding to know what the hell you thought you were doing, like a tired and cranky mom, back in the Yukon Protectorate.

Afia grinned and pointed her scanner at the door controls, having stepped back into gravity to let it keep her still. The rest were watching or organizing gear so that it wouldn't float off. Javier was close, but off to one side, parallaxing on her with his own gear from the other side of that line.

They'd keep beaming everything back to Del and Suvi constantly, as long as they could. She had the processing power to track it all and see things that mere mortals might miss.

If there were any such creatures with Afia today.

She snickered.

"What?" Javier asked quietly.

"You don't gotta be crazy to enjoy this…" she said.

"But it helps," he finished for her. "Anything worth mentioning?"

"Live systems after however long," she said. "Worth something to someone. Kinda like we were back at *A'Nacia* in the mine field."

"Thinking the same thing," he said. "We'll wait for Death to be ready before we go anywhere."

"I'm always ready," Djamila chimed in with a grin in her voice.

"The rest might need a few seconds," Javier retorted.

Afia grinned but kept quiet. Short of something exploding, she was in the safest spot she could be in, with so many gunners handy, all keyed up.

But this was her show. Even Javier was only along for his scientific expertise, like Nikos. Her and Ilan had point until Djamila had a reason to shoot somebody. She turned and found Ilan in her wingwake, just waiting, that goofy grin on his face shining through his shield.

He nodded, multitool in one hand. Wasn't the best tool for any single job, but you could do damned near anything with it, from prying shit open to backing out bolts to bashing shit with four kilos of hull-grade alloy.

Boy carried it like a teddy bear, but she was frequently the same with her portable sensor, so she wasn't about to say anything.

They approached the door that looked like a fairly standard design for an airlock. At least according to the earliest chapters in *So You Want To Be An Engineer?*. Standard tenkey pad using Arabic numbers.

She was still waiting for the day some moron had decided to get cute and do one of these things in Ancient Chinese or something.

Ten keys in four rows of three each. Older than starflight. Zero centered bottom, flanked by red and green buttons. Afia had no idea what those bottom buttons did because solar radiation from somewhere had faded them to pretty much nothing.

"Suvi, I'm scanning something that needs false color analysis," she said, pointing her portable at it and taking a stable picture. "Please identify any faded markings and language."

You were supposed to etch the metal for exactly this reason, but this ship might also be several thousand years old, back before they had learned those lessons. Or maybe *why* they learned them.

"Stand by," Suvi replied. "Arabic number pattern as standard. Red appears to be bay door controls. Green is airlock."

"What language?" Javier asked.

"English, of all things," Suvi replied with a laugh. "Old English. Space Age stuff, rather than starflight era."

Weird, but nobody was paying Afia to be a linguist. She had three and a half of those behind her. Javier could make do, but Nikos and Bethany were much better.

"Okay, everyone," Afia announced. "I am about to see if the airlock doors will work after this long. Stand by and pay attention in case something happens."

She turned and nodded to Ilan to move in with her. She reached into a pouch and pulled out a sprayer with the best lubricating gunk in the galaxy. Got into any crack and kinda ate the top level of grime, metal, or rust, which was usually just what you needed with old metal parts left in the solar wind too long.

Or galactic wind. Whatever this ship had flown through.

A thought struck her.

"Suvi, we haven't seen anything like weapon turrets or missile bays on that smooth exterior, have we?" she asked.

"Negative, Afia," the woman replied. "Been pinging. My drone reports nothing like that inside your bay, either."

Huh.

"Thank you."

She moved close and studied the hatch. Looked like the kind that rolled inward on big hinges, to slam shut like a cork in a bottle if you had a decompression event.

"Ilan, I'm going to hit the entire frame," she announced

to the team. "We'll wait a minute, then you'll bang it once with your wrench. Hopefully, that will break everything loose."

"Gotcha," the man said.

Two syllables, which was one more than she expected. Boy was quiet when he was in the field.

She went to work, nailing all the gaps with goop. Then she nodded and Ilan spanged the hull once.

No air, but she felt it in her shoes. He'd put his shoulders into that one.

"Suvi, any response?" she asked the drone floating nearby.

The armed one with good sensors ramped up to paranoid, looking at this ship.

"Negative on all channels, Afia."

So far, so good.

She moved to the panel and scanned it. Some power there, but not much. Probably waiting for her to close a connection.

"Trying the controls now," she announced.

Green button.

Here goes nothing.

PART FIVE

J avier watched, standing off to one side, out of the way of Djamila and her gun team. The other two scientists were off with him, but back some, just to be safe.

Afia was doing her thing. That was why she was here, so he didn't interfere. Technically, he wasn't the Science Officer anymore, but it was his ship and mission, so nobody got to tell him to stay back and read.

Nobody.

For a long moment, nothing happened, then the airlock hatch jarred once and started inward. Broken free from the tack welds a solar wind can create, and power moving the heavy thing in.

Big. Maybe eight centimeters thick, with a ring around the edge where it seated properly.

"Moving in to confirm the airlock," Afia said.

Javier had a slanted view, but he saw lights come on. And the ship had some level of atmosphere contained inside, as well as power. Creator only knew what you might find.

He wanted to be the one to go in first, but that was him.

Javier was willing to admit now that sending his own men in to die in a reactor leak had done more damage to him than he'd known how to handle emotionally. That it was Afia and Ilan, two of his closest friends, going in, sent him into uncomfortable flashbacks.

He worked on his breathing.

You okay? Medical readings moving off baseline.

Times Square Marquee on the inside of his helmet. Someone watching his bio readings and poking him. But Suvi was like that.

He keyed a private channel to her.

"Bad memories," he said quietly.

"That's why I was watching," she replied. "I've heard your nightmares."

Even he didn't really remember them that well these days, but she'd been there when he'd been at his worst.

"Thank you," he said.

Not much more to say. It was enough that she cared.

He had friends. What person could really say that?

"Okay, folks," Afia called. "We're going to try to lock into the ship itself. Djamila, we've got space for you and one other in this lock. Plus the drone."

"Sascha," the Dragoon said without hesitation.

Javier watched the two women and Suvi enter and then the door began to close.

"Sealing up now," Afia kept a running commentary going. "Lights are on, but about half appear dead at present."

Javier moved up to where he was closer to the door. With Djamila across the wall, technically he was the next ranking officer present. Time to earn his money.

"We are sealed," Afia said. "Gooping the inner door now and we'll try that next. Controls on the wall confirm an atmosphere over on the other side, but not the status. Javier, we'll need you scanning it before anyone tests."

He grunted. Standard procedure. You never trusted a derelict. Everyone here had thirty or more hours of power left in their skinsuits, plus the gun bunnies had brought several recharger packs. They could stay aboard for a week before they ran out of food and power.

He absolutely knew that he'd have his answers long before then.

The wait was like water torture. Drips falling slowly on his forehead without pattern or letup.

He'd been through worse.

"Okay, inner hatch is opening," Afia said. "Smoother. Suvi and Sykora are moving into position. Stand by. We have atmosphere here, but not at a sufficient pressure for anyone to be outside suits for long, so everyone assume you are staying bottled up until Javier or I tell you otherwise."

There was a long pause as that inner hatch opened and everyone settled. Javier could see it in his mind: Suvi on point riding her lifters out into the space and pinging hard, turret deployed and ready to thump a moose upside the head.

Everyone else would remain in the airlock until Suvi said to move, then Djamila and Sascha would step out, guns out and safeties off. Ilan and Afia wouldn't be cleared to emerge until nothing jumped out.

He waited.

"Oh, shit," someone muttered. Female voice, but hardly a whisper, so he couldn't say who it was. "Wait until Javier sees this."

Which was an exceptionally rude thing to say over an open comm, especially when he was about fifteen meters away, separated by a lot of metal that would keep him from seeing anything.

"Okay, folks, we're safe," Afia said now. "Inner portion of the ship is kind of like a sporting arena, with ziggurat steps down to a bowl that is a significant portion of the center of the ship. Think *Shangdu*, but instead of a lake you have a…I guess we'd call it a forest. Something. Gonna need a Science Officer botanist and his official opinions. Do not see anything moving around right now, but that's not proof. We're on a deck. Maybe I'd call it a promenade. Reminds me of those ancient, Roman houses where you had rooms around the outside, then a deck, then a central courtyard. Dragoon?"

"Go ahead," Djamila said.

"Okay," Afia said now. "Javier, you, Bethany, Nikos, and about half the gun bunnies can fit through. The other half to remain out in the flight bay for now as a ready reserve in case we need something. *Excalibur*, how is our signal?"

"Some lag," Suvi said. "Some static. Recommend boosters on the inside of the airlock and outside for now, just to maintain stable communications. The hull composition is not an alloy I am familiar with, but it's not interfering too much with most of our channels. Anything at the low end would be blocked pretty solid."

Javier nodded. You wanted X-rays and stuff at that end of the spectrum to be stopped as much as possible, while radio and the other end was allowed through. All starships did it that way, but this went back thousands of years, and represented a culture that had faded from galactic history, as far as he knew. *Trotau Skale* notwithstanding.

He moved to the airlock, signaling the others. Hajna and three of the goons brought their heavy packs with them. Iqbal, Galal, and Helmfried joined him, leaving Heydar, Demyan, and Tom as the backup team. As far as Javier was concerned, they were all interchangeable, other than Helmfried was the best medic. Iqbal might be smarter than the others by a bit, but none of them were dumb.

Just linear and violent as a first resort rather than last.
He had better ways to solve the galaxy's problems.
They got in and he keyed the airlock closed.

KIMMERIA

PART ONE

Kiliyn was still nearly beside himself with rage, seated in the lounge of the vessel and watching nearby stars. He worked to control himself, outwardly calm as always, but it was a lie.

His anger wanted to consume him. Had since he had pretended to be an old associate of both Javier Aritza and Nikos Askvig, only to discover that the former had indeed been here and apparently contracted the latter.

Possibly raced off to steal his prize in the process.

Kiliyn found it wise that he had decided that Milya was better in command. She had taken all of his information and immediately done two things. First, she had stopped looking for something small with which they might sneak out and locate their target.

Second, she had contacted The Belfast Group Holding Company and given them enough information to get their attention. They were not one of Jarre Foundation's mortal enemies. Not like Walvisbaai.

At the same time, nobody around here was. Belfast were pirates and smugglers, but professional enough to sign contracts that Kiliyn expected to be honored. He had never known that *Trotau Skale* had the resources to locate and recover the ancient vessel that had been their tribe's home for so long.

If they had been able to find it, they would have required the assistance of someone to help them salvage the ship. Belfast had a pretty good reputation with that sort of thing.

And Milya had made certain to send detailed reports to the elders via multiple channels, just so they knew what had happened, what he suspected, and where to look if something might happen to him and Milya.

He looked up at the sound of the hatch opening. Milya and Captain London Avison, commander of this vessel, the Belfast Holdings Corsair *Adamant Capital.*

He rose and studied the woman. Milya had been selected for this mission because she did not stand out. Captain Avison would command any room she entered.

Short, or perhaps just average in height. She had broad shoulders like a man and a squarish torso that did not pinch in at the waist or flare out at the hips. Black hair, straight and pulled back into a tail with a band. Dark eyes that had seemed shrewd or cruel since he first met her, depending on the moment.

Still, one of their connections, though he had never intended to bring Belfast in this soon. Nor to ask them to send a warship.

Captain Avison took a seat and smiled as he and Milya joined her.

"We'll be underway in about an hour," she said.

For such a hard-looking woman, she had a quiet, seductive voice that you might hire to read the news on a radio broadcast. Kiliyn could not help but be drawn to it.

Probably not an accident on her part. The woman was a pirate captain. Or close enough to paint with the same brush.

"Thank you," Kiliyn replied, nodding. "You are familiar with the vessel we chase?"

"I am not, but we've heard the reports from *Nidavellir*, and what they did to Walvisbaai," Avison said. "*Adamant Capital* cannot match such a vessel in combat. Even with surprise, they are far outside our league."

Kiliyn turned to Milya for help. She had negotiated this deal. He was only in charge on paper at this point, so that the elders would not be offended at someone else issuing orders.

"We will pursue," Milya interjected. "If they have not found the ship, then we stand a chance of getting there first."

"And if they have?" he asked, turning to look at both women.

Captain Avison smiled grimly.

"Then we might just have to destroy it." Milya's smile matched the Captain's.

Had he come all this distance, just to fail at the end?

PART TWO

J avier was first of the group out of the airlock because damn it, he was going to be first. Nikos and Bethany were close behind, but there were already three killers over there, plus Afia and Ilan, so it wasn't like there was anybody going to jump out and hurt him.

The stupid inner hatch seemed to be mocking him with how slowly it opened, but he took a breath and realized just how hyped he was that there was a project over here requiring a professional botanist.

He'd done a lot of stupid (and occasionally illegal) things in his time. Very few of them had required botany.

Not none. Just few.

So he was vibrating at a higher pitch than normal. The Times Square Marquee came live again.

You're hyperventilating, she reminded him.

Javier realized it, slowed his breathing, and focused on returning to the normal flow of time.

The hatch swung inward and he caught sight of the thing that had gotten Afia to attach a charging circuit directly to his adrenal gland.

Shit.

Life. Sort of.

Hajna put a hand on his kidneys and shoved him into the hallway, because he'd frozen in place in the doorway.

Javier stumbled forward a bit and then just went ahead and walked to the edge of the platform, the others falling in beside and around him.

They were on a third-floor mezzanine ring that ran all the way around the outside of the basin below him. Javier would call it a valley. Maybe that park they occasionally built in the middle of a city, wrapping a huge building around it.

Huge indeed.

Behnam's lake, aboard her ship, was comparable in scale. But hers was just water. This had been a park.

Autonomous fingers brought his scanner around and started to work.

Atmospheric pressure low, but they knew that. Composition heavy on the carbon dioxide and nitrogen end. Hardly any oxygen. Gravity at twelve percent. Temperature a little above freezing, but not much.

In his mind's eye, he saw someone standing on this very spot, two thousand years ago as they waved goodbye to everything and hoped that the systems would hold out until they returned.

Because it was obvious that nobody lived here today.

Nikos and Bethany were on his right, but he turned to Djamila. And Suvi.

"Evolutionary pressures have been at work," he said simply. "Closed environment like this will produce an island effect on whatever animal forms remained behind, but that just means fast and dangerous, instead of big and mean. Alternatively, if there were no predators, you'll eventually speciate into two groups, but I have no idea what they started with. Omnivores would be the best candidate for that."

"Pollinators?" Djamila asked.

"Presumably," he agreed. "I have my bees, but I also hand pollinated things instead of dealing with hummingbirds. I would want insects, ground and aerial if I was doing this. By now, they will have colonized every spot they could get to. Assuming they could. Suvi, now that we have heavy teams handy, I want you to do a quartering overflight of the basin, scanning absolutely everything and transmitting it back to yourself for analysis. Ask Rainier for help. Nobody goes down there until we know what we're dealing with."

Djamila nodded and began making complicated gestures to her team, getting a perimeter set up.

Javier turned and looked up. Three more levels above them, but one of the guys had a weapon pointed that direction.

Suvi went straight up, which would help, as she could cover everything in here just fine. He turned to Nikos now and caught the way the man's eyes were almost as big as Javier's felt.

"Welcome to *Kimmeria*, Nikos," he said.

PART THREE

Djamila didn't have nearly the resources handy to handle a task like this correctly. On the other hand, it would have required her to spend several months sifting through candidates to find the hundred men and women she would have brought with her on a mission whose scope and complexity had just exploded around her.

She had herself and her two pathfinders, to five people. Suvi would be covering in armed overwatch. The three men would be holding the edges and she needed the other three outside, against whatever surprises might want to sneak up on them.

Still, she had experts. The risks had been mitigated as well as she could, and there were other crew members who could be brought over from the ship, once she had neutralized threats.

"We'll set up a base of operations here," Djamila announced. "Suvi, check the steps above us please."

A beep answered, and a map began to fill in as the drone's sensors started working.

Djamila would assign some level of arboreal nature to

whatever life had survived this long. There were trees down there, of a sort. More evergreen than anything, but not species she could distinguish. Needles on narrow boles, rather than leaves that could fall in an autumn that might never come.

Audio sensors did not identify anything remotely like birdsong, but that meant nothing at this range, as some sort of passive life support had been working well enough to keep everything alive this long.

She turned and walked close to Javier, even though she could have just yelled across the radio.

"I'd like three teams," she said.

Better to ask politely and get him to buy off than having the man argue with her and do it his own way.

"Agreed," he nodded up at her. "Afia and Bethany. Ilan and Nikos. And me."

Djamila considered the breakdown. Strong engineer and hopeless academic with each group, but Bethany and Afia had a distinct edge there for survival capabilities.

"Sascha, you accompany Ilan and Nikos," she announced. "Hajna, you will be with Afia and Bethany. I'll try to keep the Science Officer from getting into too much trouble."

The amount of laughter on the line was gratifying. Nobody could keep Javier in line, possibly including himself. Having her along would give him the best chance.

"Transmitting map updates now," Suvi said over the line. "All hands note that there are six exits from each promenade level. Bow and stern, plus sixty and one hundred thirty degrees down each flank, following the egg shape of the outer hull. We are also off-center forward, so I am including a large volume of blank space presumably representing engines and control spaces."

Djamila brought up controls to play with the map

updates. As always, excellent, because she and Suvi had sat down one day and worked it all out, those details that Djamila needed in order to work.

Working with professionals. Almost enough to make her smile.

"Teams One, Two, and Three will move aft and look for access," she announced, pointing to herself, then Afia, then Ilan to number them. "Base team will maintain operations here and act as a mobile reserve. Keep in radio contact with all teams at all times."

"Understood, Team One," Zakhar came on the line now. "Be careful."

Djamila smiled in the hidden confines of her helmet. All those years wasted because she'd been afraid to approach him, while he'd been too busy being the captain in charge. They were making up for it, slowly.

And Zakhar Sokolov would move heaven and earth if something threatened her. Useful, when he had a warship.

She gestured folks into motion. Javier fell in on her left. Suvi was watching from her spot overhead as she mapped and looked for any sort of dangerous lifeforms.

Djamila wasn't worried about snakes. It would be small, fast things with poison that were territorially hostile, like wolverines. Anything else she could stun and hope they survived.

Or not.

They had entered the third ring at the starboard rear portal, which led only to a flight bay. Still, that gave her a good understanding of the depth of hull involved. Presumably, there would be hallways running in annular rings, buried in the outer sections, but they needed to know what was controlling this ship.

And how dangerous it might think it was.

PART FOUR

Bethany followed the others, contained in a safe cocoon of armed women and dangerous engineers. Not the worst way to go through life.

It was something of a hike to get to the aft portal, but Djamila, Javier, and Suvi kept up a running commentary on the forest. Bethany didn't do botany, but she was probably second or third best educated on the topic in this group, depending on how much Nikos had gotten outside of his core competency.

If she was following the chatter, the trees were just barely hanging on in the combination of low temperature, strange atmosphere, and broken-down systems. She'd studied enough evolutionary theory to understand that trees change much slower than animals might. Suvi had noted movement, once she hung perfectly still, but nothing had come out to say hello.

According to Javier, that suggested predators in the forest, preying on the others. However, he also said they were likely omnivores, so more like raccoons than anything.

She wondered if the island environment would create pressures for intelligence, or eliminate them. A slowly dying vessel—and the atmosphere with it—wouldn't help, if you didn't have the brains to figure out controls and tools.

She had a 3D map of the place, and that was enough for now. Later, presumably, the botanical team would want to emerge on the first ring and approach. For now, they were thirty meters above the ground, roughly.

Bethany wondered how many decks were contained in the outer section of the hull, if the rings were fifteen meters apart in elevation. That was a lot of volume to use.

This was an incredibly huge vessel, even today.

Finally, they arrived at the centerline rear hatch. The one everyone assumed went to the engines.

"Suvi, how much volume is there on the bow portion?" she asked, mostly out of curiosity.

The map on her heads-up-display changed, zooming and turning.

"Thoughts?" she asked.

The others had stopped to look at her, except for where Afia and Ilan were busy studying the hatch, with Djamila covering them.

"Old naval architectural," Bethany mused. "Bridge forward, engines aft. Mostly because that was how big cargo haulers have pretty much always done it. You want to push. At the same time, you need to see where you are going."

"You think the bridge is forward?" Javier asked. "I'm thinking aft, but clear up top."

"Top hull is curved," she reminded him. "And we didn't see any towers, although a telescoping one might be cool. If you are just watching on screens, it could be anywhere, but I'd want to look at space as I flew."

"Andak Luo and his submarine?" Djamila asked without turning her head back.

"Something like that," Bethany replied. "Would that suggest recreational facilities forward, away from all the noise and smell of engine rooms? Maybe where important people slept? We don't know them culturally, except what we can infer from their architectural decisions. They thought big and built big, but didn't have the ability to build ships that could think for themselves. At the same time, the ship's interior has a rather elegant aesthetic going, curves and smoothness over squares of any kind."

"Interesting theory, but we need life support and engines first," Javier said. "Art appreciation and museum tours can wait until later, and we don't have the staff to be two places at once."

Bethany nodded. Not surprising. Mostly, she'd been thinking out loud, when it was possible to do that around senior officers and not get into trouble, itself a novel concept.

"Stand by for dual probe launch," Captain Sokolov suddenly filled the line. "Bracketing survey coming up."

It took her a moment to translate that. Two probes, launched on a plane with the ship, but twenty degrees right and left of flight.

Oh, he was putting one at each end of the vessel so he could see engines as well as looking for the sorts of long, glass windows that would let them look in on the lost world.

She'd spent most of her career in a navy that was shrinking from budget cuts. It was strange to just be able to do something like that because it sounded like a good idea, instead of convincing a budgeting committee to pursue it.

She wasn't in the navy anymore. Not like that.

"Hey folks, I don't want to interrupt your party, but we've got the hatch controls figured out," Afia announced, drawing all eyes back around to where she and Ilan were working.

Bethany wished, for the briefest moment, that she had a

weapon to draw, just to give herself something to do. Or a sensor pack like Afia and Javier carried. She had a stunner, but now was not the time to pull it out. She just had to relax with Nikos and watch the others work.

And look for buried treasure.

PART FIVE

Nikos felt the way his cheek muscles hurt from the grin that had not left his face in hours. He wondered if Javier and the others understood what a once-in-a-lifetime moment this was.

At the same time, some of the whispers he had heard from the crew suggested that they did things on this monumental scale regularly enough to become *blasé* about it. Nikos wasn't sure if that was better or worse.

They were actually standing inside a starship that had been abandoned for perhaps a thousand years, having been launched a thousand or more before that.

Nikos fell into line, behind the tall pathfinder Hajna Flores and next to Bethany, as the team of Afia Burakgazi and Ilan Yu prepared to open the door.

There were many more guns in evidence than he would have expected, but again, they did this more often, and obviously had entirely different opinions on how to approach it from a middle-aged academic.

But he was here.

"Okay, triggering override now," Afia announced,

stepping to one side and leaving Ilan and his meter-long wrench closest to the opening.

Nothing jumped out as the door slid sideways into the wall. The air did puff a little bit, but that just let him know that it had been sealed before this. Nikos could see a short corridor headed inward to terminate at a second such hatch, so presumably something of an airlock seal had been maintained.

He wasn't a ship builder, but so much volume behind him argued for keeping personnel quarters and such safe, in case something did penetrate. Most ships were interrupted regularly by reinforced sections, especially to handle damage in a vacuum.

Afia, Ilan, and Dragoon Sykora moved into the hallway. Nikos estimated it at roughly fifteen meters deep and three wide and tall. Not standards in use today, but regular enough to have been a design decision. In fact, the promenade levels were fifteen meters elevation apart.

Everything done in multiples of threes? Interesting.

He pulled out a small datapad and added more observations. He wasn't constantly writing down every little thing, because the flying machine Suvi was using had mapping scanners, and both Javier and Afia had portable units.

Plus, he would be interviewing everyone during their down time. Still, three-meter building blocks, as it were, suggested something that he needed to notate.

Excellent.

"Okay, we're assuming airlock-quality work here," Ilan announced, breaking his usual silence. "Outer hatch is facing you folks and the forest. Inner is to the quarters. We're going to close this hatch before opening the next one."

"Bethany, Nikos, and Hajna join us," Sykora ordered.

"Sascha, you have overwatch until we know what we're facing here."

Everyone moved and sorted themselves out. It did not help that only Afia Burakgazi was shorter than him among this group, so Nikos was spending a lot of time craning around shoulders and elbows to see anything.

Once it was determined to be safe, he would no doubt be free to explore more, presumably with Bethany and Hajna. Then he could start making useful observations and discoveries.

Patience.

They got into the hallway and Ilan closed them in. Afia opened the other side, and again there was a small poof of air. Higher pressure on the engines side. Considering that the arboretum was at exceptionally low atmospheric pressure, that boded well for perhaps one day being able to create a livable environment in this ship again.

Nikos Askvig wasn't the sort of glory hound that pursued things just to see his name on the front page, but he had no doubt that the joint history of this ship that he would eventually write up with Leonora would be the capstone of both of their careers.

He found himself looking forward to it.

Beyond, they found a darkened hallway, just as the others had estimated. No lights at all, save what they had on their helmets and left wrists.

"Javier, a note," he said with a hint of diffidence that got the man to turn back. "Everything appears to be done in multiples of three meters as a measuring unit. This hallway. The promenade widths and levels. Perhaps the rooms we encounter will be arranged as such as well?"

"Good catch, Nikos," the man nodded. "Not sure what it will mean, but it gives us a starting point. Djamila?"

The Amazonian woman stepped out and looked both

ways, pistols one hundred and eighty degrees apart, but held with such certainty that Nikos just knew the woman could see with her ears to shoot.

She gave off that air. Hajna moved next, the two women now back-to-back as the rest of the survey team moved into the corridor.

Again, three meters wide, three meters tall. Curved slightly, as one would expect from the inner and outer shapes. Artistic, in ways he wasn't used to, on any ship.

Javier looked right and left like a man crossing a busy street against ground vehicles. He nodded and gestured left for reasons Nikos wasn't privy.

The entire team moved down about fifteen meters (*a-ha!*) and ended up at another hatch.

"Bethany, Nikos, you're on," Javier said, tapping a placard about shoulder height to the right of the doorway.

Nikos recognized the words, only because Suvi had suggested Terrestrial English originally. The ancient tongue.

Such a language still existed, but folks from that era would be largely lost, today not just because of the drift of accents over time, but from the way the language itself had continued to accrete words and concepts.

Seven major languages had largely become dominant in the modern era, all much modified: English, Spanish, Hindi, Mandarin, Arabic, Kiswahili, and Bulgarian. At the same time, the mass colonization over the last four thousand years had introduced new fusions and even a few created languages.

Nikos found himself looking forward to finding a long-written passage somewhere, just because he was fairly certain that he could more accurately date the launch of this ship, and its subsequent isolation from exterior cultural influences, by the linguistic structure.

All that time spent in libraries did yield some benefit, after all.

"Javier, this announces the main engine rooms and access to starboard auxiliary power reactors," Nikos said. "It also includes radiation warnings and demands that only authorized crew may enter the space."

"As the new commander of this vessel, I duly authorize all of you," he said with a laugh. "There you go. Afia, what's the count?"

Nikos watched as Afia and Ilan huddled over their portable scanner units for a long moment. He watched past them, around the curve towards the forward bits of the ship. He shined his lights forward, supplementing Hajna's but not really cutting deeper.

Dust. Dust?

Oh, yes, of course. Biological materials would get into the air and be blown about, to eventually land. He could only imagine what the air filtration units would look like at this point. Perhaps they had grown completely over with gunk? That would explain much.

"Hajna, we are leaving tracks," he noted.

"Absolutely, Doc," she agreed with a happy voice. "Nothing else is. At least at present."

"Are we expecting anything?"

"We are not, Nikos," Djamila spoke. "However, until we have swept the vessel entirely, it behooves us to be careful. Hopefully, we will be able to activate lights shortly."

He nodded and stepped clear as the experts went to work.

What other secrets might this ancient vessel yield?

PART SIX

J avier had flashbacks to sneaking aboard *Hammerfield* that first time, expecting something to wake up and start shooting at him. Or send maintenance robots and other nightmares chasing him through the corridors and decks.

His nightmares had been bad enough lately, thank you very much.

"Javier, we're not reading anything above normal through the hatch," Afia said. "Granted, won't mean anything until we open it."

"Agreed," he replied. "Everyone back towards the bottom of the egg. When you open it, you step back as well until we're sure nothing will happen. Djamila and the girls can be prepared for that. Ilan'll stick his sensor probe around the corner to watch."

"Is it worth bringing Suvi down?" Djamila asked.

Of course the dragoon would want more firepower. Probably already regretting not having an entire battalion of shock troops handy to invade the place. That was how she thought.

"No, I want her completing a survey and covering our line of retreat," he replied in a serious voice, with the grin only in his eyes at turning the tables on her. "We'll do this patiently. I only have about five questions I need answered here, then we'll head back, possibly all the way to *Excalibur* entirely and plot our next moves."

He glanced over and caught the blink of surprise in her eyes. Javier, being careful? What was the galaxy coming to?

Except that everyone knew he had a reason to survive now. Well, two, but Suvi was going to outlive him anyway, like she had her first captain, Ayumu Ulfsson, a century ago. And she had her own warship.

He fully intended to make it back to *Altai*. If that meant not taking stupid chances, so be it.

Not everything had to be to the death, after all.

Everyone rearranged. He was in the middle with Afia, Bethany, and Nikos. Hajna ended up tail gunner, so Sascha and Djamila were covering Ilan as he pried the doors then got them rolling once he had broken loose junk welds.

The joys of goop.

"Okay, stand by for scan," Ilan said as he shifted things around, once no monsters decided to come out and eat everybody.

Ilan and that meter of hullmetal wrench were the reason the boy was on point rather than Afia, after all. Lot of things you could do with that much torque.

"Huh," Ilan said after a few moments. "I'm catching elevated radiation levels, but also a really weird mix of isotopes in the air. Off-beat half-lives. Nothing immediately dangerous, but don't breath it and we'll need to wash the surfaces of the suits when we get home. If I had to guess, I'd say we had a reactor malfunction at some point and a relatively recent explosion subsequent back there. Something was on baseline load and the failsafes didn't react fast enough."

Javier remembered a dead Norwegian rat, stuck in a transverse coolant pipe, and the all-thumbs kid he had spent about six hours talking through the repair and maintenance of the generator that had caused the grief.

Any resemblance to the man currently discussing reactor behavior in criticality incidents was purely coincidental.

But Ilan had grown up, too, from that skinny punk teaching himself how to be a machinist's mate to nearly Afia's peer in all things. Certainly Andreea Dalca, the Chief Engineer on paper, was probably already in the rearview mirror with those two. But Andreea never wanted to have any adventures at all. She was content down with her engines, coaxing them along and not having to talk to organic beings.

An introvert's introvert.

"Stick your head in and make sure, but don't linger or enter," Javier instructed him. "I'm coming up as well."

He nodded to Djamila, just because there was no way in hell she wouldn't come.

Ilan had craned his head in and looked. Javier crossed to the far side of the door itself and let Djamila stand in the center, both pistols aimed into the room like she did.

"Yup," Javier agreed. "Yuck. Number four back on the right?"

"Looks like it," Ilan said. "Nothing floating around indicates a full meltdown. More like a coolant system breached inside somewhere and has let air hit metals. Cold enough here to keep it from full vaporizing, but that's partly the reason that the air is warmer on this side of the door. Gonna need a remotely piloted vehicle to get in and see what it is. Even Suvi's drones would likely short-circuit as she gets close to the radiation."

"You figure out how to build and fly one," Javier said.

He flipped his scanner to camera mode and pinged the entire inside of the vast space. Sixty meters deep was his guess, and then only because Nikos said multiples of three. Maybe forty-five meters tall, with open-grate catwalks around various machines that looked like mountain trolls squatting down on a cold night.

Or something equally weird. What had they used to do this? Obviously something with one hell of a long half-life, to still be putting out power after this much time.

Nine things down each side that he figured were reactors from the way they were arranged. Power generators, rather than engines. Three of those in the center, but obviously cold.

Most likely off, if he had to guess, as the outer tubes were either closed or used some weird venting system he hadn't figured out.

"Zakhar, you reading me?" he asked now.

"Patchy," came a staticky reply, which told Javier just how much radiation there was in the room.

"Three engines, dead aft, centered on the plane with where we entered," Javier said. "You see anything?"

"Stand by."

Javier let his handheld nag him that he needed to step back and shower to get nasty particles off his skin, but the suit was fine. Worst thing that might happen was this one got too much and he tossed it into space.

The Science Officer had brought a LOT of spares with him, knowing how he was.

"Javier, three small tubes visible aft," Zakhar said now over the interference. "Ambient temperature."

"Good enough," Javier said. "Withdrawing now. Ilan, close her up."

He stepped back and watched his other sidekick elbow the door controls. They had been gooped well, because they slammed shut now like a bank vault.

You wanted that in engineering. Kept radiation leaks on the other side of the wall. Like now.

"I didn't see anything like life support generators," he said, turning to Djamila and the others. "Even those plants probably aren't sufficient, unless they got heavily modified at the beginning."

"Why wouldn't they have been?" the tall woman asked.

Why not indeed?

"Dunno," he shrugged. "Want to withdraw now to our base camp and review a few things. Maybe use some of our spare water to wipe you, me, and Ilan down against radiation. We'll see when we get there."

The others weren't sure what was up, but they didn't have all the parts of this whole in their heads. Came of specializing, when he'd spent the last decade or more as a generalist.

It had kept him alive.

Back around the curve. They airlocked through, just to keep any air from circulating right now. All of the gunbunnies on this side were intact, plus Suvi beeped loudly from overhead as a way of saying hello.

"Suvi, anything larger than a housecat?" he asked as they emerged and Ilan closed the hatch behind him.

"Nope," she replied. "Islander-scaled versions of something that might be a wallaby."

Shit, he hadn't even considered *Earth* biology in the mess. He'd just automatically assumed Englishers had grabbed critters from home or North America, but Australia was also a former colony if you went back far enough.

"Tree-climbing kangaroo?" he asked.

"*Macropodidae* includes *Dendrolagus ursinus*," she replied. "Ursine or white-throated tree-kangaroo, depending on the writer. These are half the size they get on *Earth* but look like them."

"Encyclopedia?" he asked, intrigued now.

Was this an ark gone wrong, too?

"Arboreal," she said. "Nocturnal. Marsupial. Vegetarian. Possibly moving to omnivorate, over time, but I'd have to see evidence."

"Assume something cleans up corpses," he replied automatically. "Ants or beetles. And eventually you need an apex predator."

"Affirmative," she said. "Haven't seen anything, but that's not the same."

"How's your mapping coming?" he asked as the group started walking around the promenade.

"Ready to name the trees," she said with a laugh.

"Good," he decided. "Join us back at base for now, but I might leave you here overnight when we head home."

"Gotcha."

It all felt right. At the same time, something felt off and he didn't know what it was.

The ship had secrets. That much he was certain. Something had caused a group to depart for *Trotau Skale*. Presumably all of them. Or all the survivors.

Maybe that was it? Something had gone wrong and folks had fled to the nearest empty world they could find, fully intent on returning. Then something went wrong there, too?

Yeah. That felt better.

Trotau Skale was poor. If the survivors had landed on a metal-poor world, they might have fallen back to primitive pretty fast. Then needed help from folks around them that they saw as barbarians.

Plunderers that they would have to hide *Kimmeria* from.

An insular people, proud with ancient traditions, but only now in a position to return to Avalon and look for King Arthur?

Javier held that as a working hypothesis for now.

He still had several more mysteries to solve.

PART SEVEN

Afia had pulled everything off everybody's portable scanners and merged it into a single dataset while Javier argued with Djamila and Zakhar. Weirdly, Nikos was on Javier's side that they needed to return fully to *Excalibur* and spend a couple of days preparing for a return.

Patient scholars versus former pirates, she supposed.

Ilan had been right about the one reactor breaching. But she guessed it had been fully banked at the time. Maybe the act of the control systems trying to bring it up in sequence had caused the incident? Then the control systems had bypassed it and moved on to number five on that side, keeping four permanently out of the load mixture?

That suggested a pretty good autonomous system. Not too smart, or it might have realized that the reactor was iffy and skipped it anyway, but Afia wasn't sure any system except Suvi would have been able to make that kind of intuitive leap.

Even her so-called cousins weren't that sharp.

"Whatchagot?" Ilan asked on a private line.

Afia explained her logic.

"Solid," he agreed.

High praise from the man. The definition of *taciturn* in the dictionary included a cute line drawing of Ilan Yu.

"So maybe we need to do two things?" he continued. "Find a way to scram it hard. Maybe permanently. Then a way to seal off wherever it's leaking. Scrammed, the temp will drop and we won't have to worry about pressure building up. At that point, we kick the fans on in there. Wait a day and then go in with the same robots to scrape all the gunk off the air filters and just eject it directly into space?"

"Not before?" Afia asked, mostly just testing the boy.

He was sharp as a knife these days. Especially when lives were at risk.

"How long have they already been accumulating?" he asked. "Doubt we're anywhere close to a dangerous concentration, but probably cooks my robot unless we add a quarter meter of insulator between the arms and the control box."

"Hull alloy tough enough for what you envision?" Afia asked.

She repaired things. He was the one that got weird with the welding laser. Part of the reason Zakhar had assigned him to Javier in the first place.

Artists.

And dorks.

She watched his eyes. And then his hands came up and started motioning, like he had three of them and was trying to undress a girl to get at the fun parts.

She grinned as he looked up at her suddenly and turned beet red. Probably been envisioning doing exactly that to her, just to confirm his controls.

Boys.

All you had to do was ask nice.

But she liked watching him turn that color.

"Think I got something," he said, biting his lip in a cute way, however unconsciously it was. "Wheels, since I got flat deck in there. Two loader arms and a bucket. Need your help figuring out the sensor array."

She nodded. He did mechanical better than anybody, but if he needed a radiation shield in place, that meant stuff sitting back on range squared or maybe even cubed, depending on the half-lives.

"Horns," she offered. "Three of them as periscopes. Two arms and a bucket, so build it on a hex and put your sensor towers in the gaps."

"Huh," he grunted. "Yeah, okay. You'll need to wire them. Not sure how to best parallax this."

"That's why Javier wants to head home," Afia reminded them. "Build stuff properly instead of trying to freelance in an atmosphere we can't breathe safely."

"Won't that take too long?" he asked.

"Ilan, it's been sitting here for thousands of years," Afia said. "Nothing interesting is scheduled to happen in the next week."

MYSTERIES

PART ONE

K iliyn was still being treated publicly like he was in charge, but that was Milya taking pains to remain in the background. Outside of their own, little conspiracy, he was still the favored one by the elders, upon whom glory or reprobation of this mission would be heaped at the end.

He knew the truth.

Today, he was on the long, skinny bridge of *Adamant Capital*, standing with one arm apparently possessively around Milya's hip, though that was mostly for show. Not that they didn't engage in marital pleasures like proper folks occasionally. However, in privacy, and usually when she initiated.

Otherwise, it felt too much like he was falling into the character the elders had chosen for him, that of a wealthy dilettante traveling with his mistress. He understood that it made a useful cover for conducting a secret mission like this, but he would still eventually return home.

Thankfully, he was not alternatively married, nor her. That might introduce...complications later.

Captain Avison was nearby, directing her crew. Kiliyn

was merely an observer. She turned to him now, as she had bought the myth and considered Kiliyn to be the one in charge.

"We have analyzed the map you produced," she said, still speaking in that quiet, seductive tone that seemed so at odds with the woman's physical appearance. "The vector begins here. Literally, as close to this spot as we could estimate, given the time lag and gravity deflections."

She raised an arm now, pointing with all of her fingers like a knife blade, rather than just one. It was a distracting mannerism.

"*Kimmeria* was projected that direction," she continued. "At present, we have a rough estimate of the speed, based on your ancient stories. My intent is to plot a jump that puts us at that location, at which time we'll be able to sit and look around, hopefully locating a nearby object moving in the correct manner. What do I not know?"

"I beg your pardon?" Kiliyn asked, confused.

Milya leaned her weight into him, just like a helpful girlfriend.

"She's told me what we're looking for," Avison said, pointing to Milya. "Given me a reproduction of the map such that we can likely track down your ship, assuming that it hasn't been destroyed or even found in the intervening centuries. What information have your elders entrusted you with that will make my searching easier or harder now? Also, what happens when we find it? What kinds of traps lie in wait?"

She waited, studying him.

Kiliyn was a bureaucrat. That was honestly the best way to describe him. Part of the inner circle of scholars of the ancients, but young enough to not be one of the decision makers. Just the son of such a man. Thus, the elders had selected him and assigned him a woman to make his travels look less suspicious.

What did Captain Avison need to know?

He turned to Milya. Saw her dark eyes look up at him with great, feigned innocence.

"Do they know the ancient tales?" he asked.

"She does not."

Kiliyn nodded. Looked around. Considered the handful of other crew members, quietly minding their stations.

He envisioned each of them as giant ears, pointed his direction. Likely they were.

But Belfast was one of the groups the elders had instructed him to contact, when it became necessary. Everything had just happened much sooner than he had expected.

What had he expected?

Kiliyn found that he didn't know. Maybe that was the source of his discomfort.

"*Kimmeria* departed *Earth* in the year 5497," he began now. It would all come out. Assuredly, it was being recorded, so he made a note to edit what he said carefully. Someone would hear every word he said now. "In 6619, the colony at *Trotau Skale* was established. In between those two dates, our ancestors traveled on the great ship."

He caught the gasps around him. On paper, it sounded simple. It was only when you considered that the tribe had successfully gone more than eleven centuries in space that the scale of the event became clear.

Kiliyn Brinov took a deep breath and consigned himself to the history books. Whatever books might be written.

"We left the ship *Kimmeria* at the end of a civil war," he continued, squeezing Milya close. "Our ancestors had fallen into two factions by that time. They had argued about rejoining society permanently, instead of just traveling to nearby systems to occasionally trade, as had been their habit for so long. They had a great technological edge on everyone else, yet some feared a hostile encounter where someone might try to overwhelm them and take the ship."

He was watching the Captain. London Avison leaned in at his words, however slightly and unconsciously.

Salvage. Plunder. Pillage. Whatever word you wanted to use. *Kimmeria* had been built as a shining city on the hill, at a time when ships were not routinely armed against folks like Walvisbaai or others.

Belfast Group were more upright than some. It was still a low bar to clear in many sectors.

"The ship was unarmed," he said, revealing the first surprise. "Secrecy and stealth had been their successful *modus operandi* for a long time. After so many centuries, they had also inbred some, but it wasn't bad because the original group had all been scientists and they had adjusted their genetics. Not to make supermen, but to eliminate recessive diseases."

"What happened at the end?" London asked now, her voice worming into his head.

"The elders argued, but could not resolve themselves," he replied, jaw clenched with the grimness of the ancient stories. "It came to open warfare, two groups literally fighting for control of the ship's destiny. Many crew members were killed before the shock of what they'd done caused the remainder to stop. To rethink. The carefully maintained society had broken down, and with it taken more than half the population. There were not enough survivors to maintain bloodlines without risk, nor to continue maintaining the ship."

"They left?" London asked.

Somehow, she had moved an entire step closer without him realizing it, until she was almost breathing on him.

"They didn't want to remain close to *Kimmeria*, given the

chance that others might find the ship," he nodded. "Instead, they sent out scouts and located *Trotau Skale*. It had been terraformed early, but never colonized, so they claimed it as their own, shuttling back and forth to deliver everything they could before abandoning the ship, seemingly forever."

"*Trotau Skale* is just about the dumbest place you could ever have picked," London said now, eyes big and inviting.

"We didn't know it at the time," Kiliyn admitted. "It looked good, but uninhabited, and my ancestors were desperate."

London nodded. She even stepped back a bit, though she pivoted on her near hip until she was still close enough that he could have put his other arm around the woman.

Was that what she was inviting?

"*Trotau Skale* hadn't been colonized because it was just barely livable," she said quietly. "Orbit's too elliptical."

"Indeed," Kiliyn agreed. "They arrived in spring. Built in summer. Then the impossibly long winter struck. Many more who had survived the war perished when suddenly they were facing winds and temperatures reminiscent of ancient Siberia, back on *Earth*. We fell from the technological heights, too proud to abandon our new world. By the time we realized we needed help, we had lost the ability to ask for it, and so my tribe eked out a living for a generation. And then a second one. Other colonists saw that we had survived, so they came. At that point, the elders instituted the Great Secret, wherein only certain folks, allied by blood and marriage, ever learned the truth of our heritage. Even today, less than a third of *Trotau Skale*'s population knows where we originally came from."

"And you chose now to find the ancient ship?" London turned her head alone to look at him.

"*Excalibur* was an outsider, just passing through this sector, so the elders made a calculated gamble," he replied.

"At some point, they must have overhead enough information to steal a copy of my map somehow, even though the seals on the container in my cabin had not been violated. They contacted the scholar Askvig, somehow finding him before I even knew he existed, and recruited the man. Now, they are looking for my ship."

"Not your ship, Brinov," London turned now to face him, her face growing hard again. "I understand that you have a historical claim, but legally, it is nothing but salvage after this long. If they find it, they might be able to keep it. That's why I'm trying to find it first. Failing that, you'll have to confront them politely, because that is a warship, and they could dismantle *Adamant Capital* like you might open a tin of beans. Is that clear?"

"It is," he replied with a sigh.

To have waited all these centuries. To have come this far.

Only to fail at the end.

Thus would his life be a mockery.

But he had no choice, save to try.

PART TWO

J avier didn't hate living in a skinsuit. At the same time, it was a lifestyle he'd be happy to avoid for the rest of his life.

They were back on *Excalibur* now. Showered and decontaminated. The radiation hadn't been all that bad, so he wasn't concerned. Mostly, it had been contained to the engine rooms, as he had expected, though the moment they cleaned the airfilters out that would change.

He arrived at the hatch he needed and pushed the button to enter. It opened and he went inside.

Machine shop. Redneck paradise, Behnam had called it on more than one occasion. Tools and machines and metal and stufffff…

Afia was seated on a chair, off to one side like she was supervising. Ilan was welding something, face mask down and bright lights arcing.

Javier gestured Afia to join him. Ilan paused long enough to flip his mask up, grin, nod, and go right back to work.

"What've we got?" he asked the woman.

"Kid's building a robot," she said with a grin.

Kid. Ilan was five years older than she was. Man was thirty-three now. But she was senior in all the ways that counted, so she could get away with it.

"Purpose?"

"According to Ilan, he thinks he can seal up the big breach, assuming no smaller ones on top we'll miss until later," she replied. "From there, the machine will pump a whole shit-ton of liquid graphite in, mixed with some things that should dampen down and absorb all the radiation, at least to safer levels. Once it hardens and fills in cracks, hopefully that reactor stops being a hotspot source and we can move on to life support. Do we know what kind of equipment they used?"

"You remember Mina's ship we found?" Javier asked. "Back at *A'Nacia*?"

"Old jalopy," Afia nodded.

"Hers was built in 7050, give or take," Javier reminded the woman. "How much better are our systems than that?"

"Lots," Afia grimaced. "How old is the beast over there?"

"Couple of millennia," Javier agreed. "Given the date, and the presumption that they were advanced for their time, I'm guessing it represents early or mid-Corporate Wars tech, in the late Resource Wars era."

"Still freaking ancient," Afia murmured.

"Plus, the trees and life have adapted to the new atmosphere, those that survived," Javier continued. "If we just shunt everything over and bring it back to normal, I'm wondering how many things we kill. Those tree-roos are probably their own species by now."

"So what do we do?" Afia looked up at him expectantly.

"Ilan's a big boy," Javier grinned. The man was taller than Javier by a shade, but nowhere near as skinny as he'd been six years ago. Grown up, as it were. "I propose him and Sascha, plus Iqbal and a few others, head aft next trip and try to scale that reactor down. You and I take Sykora forward."

"Nikos and Bethany?" Afia asked.

It was his turn to grimace.

"Bethany would prefer having fewer adventures, I think…" he started to say, but Afia's laugh cut him off.

"Oh, pretty boy, you've got a lot to learn," Afia said, placing a hand flat on his chest and laughing.

"Oh?" Javier asked.

"That girl has spent the last eight years in an abbey, being a good little nun," Afia continued. "She's ready to be a pirate now. Ready to go have the sorts of crazy adventures you and I have taken for granted, the last few years. Don't let that calm exterior fool you, buttercup."

Javier paused and reflected.

He was probably guilty of wishful thinking there. Bethany and Afia were just about the same age. Twenty-eight. At forty-three, he felt ancient by comparison.

But it was the light-years, not the days.

He'd never fooled around with Bethany Durbin. Not like he had some of the other women aboard, when they were feeling frisky. Looking back, he had possibly ignored some of Bethany's looks.

At least she'd never propositioned him directly. That might have been awkward then.

Hell, it might be awkward now. The rest of the crew were all (ex-) pirates. Bethany, like Zakhar, was *Concord* Navy. One of them. A sister in uniform, though that sort of thing hadn't stopped him when he'd worn green.

Javier took a deep breath and shook his head.

"Tomorrow," he said.

Afia nodded. The two of them had a peculiar relationship. Not like he and Behnam did, but still close. Personal. Intimate.

She knew him almost as well as Behnam and Suvi did.

"Okay, so Bethany and Nikos, with Hajna?" he asked.

She'd obviously given this a lot of thought. Smartest move on his part was to listen and learn.

"Yes," Afia smiled. "I'd bring more crew over, just so we could establish a solid pair of base camps, inside and outside. That frees up Iqbal and the boys to rearrange better, though I doubt we need forward assault teams at this point."

Javier nodded.

"How soon can you be ready for a return trip, if we don't wait for Ilan?" he asked.

"Dinner, nap, and I'm good," she said. "Call it three hours to departure?"

"Sound good," Javier replied, leaning in to kiss her on the forehead. "For everything."

She grinned and he turned to head forward. More meetings.

At least he had a better idea of what he was facing.

He hoped.

PART THREE

Djamila was in her own cabin when the door chimed, rather than meeting with Zakhar, or just relaxing in his cabin like she frequently did.

"Enter," she said, knowing that the local shard of Suvi would handle it.

Javier stepped in.

Interesting.

She had been sitting in her custom chair, knitting to relax.

"Sit," she said, pointing at the other chair.

She could keep knitting without thought for a while, just to build up the back of this sweater she was creating.

"Just talked to Afia," he began as he sat. "Ilan is building something that ought to fix the radiation problems in engineering. I'd like to leave him alone, while you, me, Afia, Nikos, Bethany, and Hajna circle forward."

"What do you expect to find?" Djamila asked.

"The power spaces are huge," he nodded. "Life support, such as it was, was partly the forest, but there should be systems forward we need to inspect. Plus, the shape of the hull suggests control spaces on the bow. Even with that semi-flattened egg shape, that's a lot of space to work with."

"How soon will Ilan be ready?" she asked.

"A day, probably," Javier said. "I'd like to go back in a couple of hours. We know what kind of environment to prepare for, so sleeping rough isn't that bad. Ilan can have Sascha follow on with him bringing over the engineering crew he needs."

Like Javier, Djamila remembered Ilan Yu on the day that fortunate soul had been assigned to a newly minted Science Officer to learn engineering. Legends of a dead rat the man had pulled out of a coolant line while fixing a generator, back on *Storm Gauntlet*. She even remembered the rat.

Today, they just assume Ilan Yu could handle those tasks. Perhaps even identify the people he needed and task them to assist.

What a strange and wonderful world.

"Is the ship safe?" Djamila asked, still knitting but feeling the twinge that reminded her she was technically unarmed right now, needles and fists and elbows notwithstanding.

"Dunno," Javier grinned. "That's why I need you and Hajna with us. Suvi has dumped a ton of information, mostly flora and exotic fauna that have survived. Nothing there looks like a threat. Mostly snakes and reptiles, none of them as big as your hand. And tree-roos."

"Australia, where marsupials originated, once had a reputation for the deadliness of anything that lived," Djamila reminded the man.

"Agreed, so my plan is to enter that ring hallway at the starboard front hatch, rather than aft," he observed. "More around that direction, hoping we can find a way to turn on any lights that work. Maybe get the airlocks to properly handle things, but I'm willing to assume that they would need to be reprogrammed to handle the forest."

"Why?" Djamila asked.

"Everything in there is surviving with a different gas mix than you and I can breathe." Javier's face turned serious now. "If we reset it, how many things die because the air is suddenly too oxygen rich? Some of those lifeforms might be unique."

Unique. What would be the value of animals that had adapted to that sort of environment, if they could transport them to a zoological facility somewhere?

Djamila knew she wasn't supposed to think like a pirate anymore, but some things had been ground deep into her bones. Even a mission for diplomacy and trade didn't remove those cold equations of profit and loss.

Still, she nodded. Pure exploration was such a novel experience for her, having been raised in a military family and a military society, even after they had lost the war.

The grinding poverty. The hopelessness. Recovering *Hammerfield* from the depths of history had lit a small spark in *Neu Berne* society, but Djamila didn't know if it would take. Or how long.

It wasn't her problem to solve. *Kimmeria* was.

"You said a couple of hours?" she circled back now.

"Afia wants to eat and nap before heading over," he nodded. "I wanted to touch base with you before announcing it generally."

She smiled. That much, the two of them had become a team, separate from all the others.

Those who willingly went into danger.

"Sounds good," Djamila decided. "The knitting can wait. You let everyone know and I will begin preparations for a larger team to join us."

He nodded and rose, departing without another word. None were needed.

Djamila stretched, put things away in their bag, and rose as well.

A shower first, just to reset her body and mind to a new day.

She knew Javier. Once over there, he would go until someone made him stop, because he wouldn't fall over for at least a day and a half.

She needed to keep up.

And she was looking forward to finding out what other secrets *Kimmeria* held.

PART FOUR

Nikos had barely stopped moving since he got back. Even sleeping was out of the question, but Leonora understood.

Now they were going back? So much to do. He'd barely managed to get his first set of notes out. Maybe he needed to ask Bethany how to set up his helmet so that he could just dictate as he went, without making everyone else listen?

Yes, that was it. He could talk to himself as he walked. Hopefully. The ancient joke came to mind, but he had no bubblegum.

"You'll be fine," Leonora said as she watched him dither.

She was seated. He had been pacing. Talking. Brain-dumping, but there was a recorder on, capturing everything, in addition to Suvi, he was certain. Leonora would absorb his words as a primary source, of course, and synthesize them into something august and scholarly. She did that.

"I'm nervous," Nikos admitted.

"How many people actually get to walk on the decks of a flying Dutchman, dear?" she asked with a grin.

Nikos had to stop and just process that. How many? How few?

"What do you suppose Javier will do with the ship?" he asked now.

"That probably depends on the things you find," she replied, eyes twinkling. "Right now, it is a lovely museum, if you could activate the engines and move it to orbit some planet. Perhaps a zoo as well, considering what Suvi has found. I'm looking forward to potentially recovering logs, as the computer systems appear to be in reasonably good shape. Imagine the stories that we will be able to tell with access to the primary sources directly."

That warmed his heart. What wonder could he extract from a thousand years in space? Or all the time before the ship was launched, which was utterly lost, as far as he knew. The organization had been deeply secretive. No records had survived on *Earth* that he had been able to locate.

Perhaps he would find enough here that a trip to the mother world would be in order? Might he know exactly where to look?

Had the secret society that had launched the ship in the first place survived, some ancient conspiracy to the *Nth* generation?

It felt so lurid. And yet, the proof was flying through space just a few dozen kilometers away, quietly crossing the darkness.

"You'll be fine, Nikos," Leonora said now, rising and embracing him.

He acknowledged that she was right. She was almost always right.

He just hoped that everything else was right, too.

PART FIVE

Bethany followed Nikos across the gap. Del still wouldn't land, but now his excuse was not knowing where the gravity wells were and not wishing to risk it.

She understood superstitions when she heard them. Del trusted that inner voice that said no. It had kept him alive several times when others hadn't been so lucky.

The group crossing was larger this trip, even without Ilan and Sascha. Ground crew, as it were, along to set up a pair of airlocked tents, inside and outside, so folks on the ship could be in shirt-sleeves environment if they wanted to. Or needed it.

Colonists, moving to claim the ship, as it were.

It was a strange feeling, doubly so for a professional historian. Bethany was used to reading about historical events, rather than initiating them.

Unbloomed rose. That was what Dorn had called her when Javier had asked. Potential, as yet unrealized.

Crossing space on a tether to invade a forgotten ship, however much they might be racing against an invisible clock until Brinov caught up with them, felt like the first warmth of spring on her skin.

She drew a heavy breath and allowed herself to relax. Touching down, she let the magnets in her boots hold her in place as she got free of the line and followed Javier and Djamila into the airlock with the others.

Only Suvi had remained behind before. She greeted them on the other side as the lock doors opened with a beeping made faint by the lack of air pressure.

"All good?" Javier asked over the comm.

"Kangaroos are inquisitive," she said. "However, to date they have not mastered the sorts of tools that would allow them to climb up to this level, even in the low gravity. Everything on the first level remains intact and sealed. Same with Two."

Bethany nodded in her helmet. Suvi had infinite patience to just fly around and inspect anything and everything, cataloging and making sure that it wasn't a threat.

And that the animals on the first deck had hopefully remained contained. How thick would the deck have to be to prevent trees from burrowing through? Javier would know. Or Rainier.

Rainier had given both her and Javier a list of things to look for. Why her, Bethany didn't know, except that the two of them were both intellectuals joined more recently to the older crew of former pirates. She brought a fresh perspective, and was used to doing research, however little of it was in the field normally.

Djamila whistled now, drawing all eyes around.

"Inside team, start setting up here," she gestured. "Overwatch as before, except that all six of you can rotate watch shifts. Exploration team will move forward and attempt to access the ring corridor from hatch starboard two. Radio communications inside have been a little weak, due to the hull itself, but this trip also includes retransmitters, so prioritize getting those up and connected to Del and *Excalibur* soonest. Questions?"

There were none. Djamila had set a high bar for recruiting anyone who operated outside the hull of *Excalibur*. You met it or you were no longer part of the team.

No bad days, as Afia liked to mutter under her breath when she thought nobody was listening.

They broke into their two groups now, Javier, Afia, and Djamila leading her and Hajna, with Nikos between them, while everybody else remained here. Suvi was with them this time, flying above and ahead. The promenade was twelve meters wide. Always multiples of three.

They had come in at the door marked three on this deck, but it was not connected to the ring corridor because of the flight deck. Walking to the forward hatch on this side took a while, mostly because they moved at a saunter, rather than a death march. That let Bethany study the forest over there.

Fir trees. She knew that after looking it up when they got back. Lights overhead in a ring that simulated a sun rising and setting. They were not as bright as she expected, but Bethany presumed that some had burned out after so long.

Would they fix them? Or merely preserve the ship in the half-broken-down state until they could rescue all the animals? Javier had been of the latter opinion. Rainier as well.

What zoo would be blessed when this was done?

She didn't see any creatures moving around as she walked, but Suvi had said that they were tiny. Island effect that shrunk them, and lack of predators, supposedly.

Bethany felt safe, considering all the predators walking with her now.

They were approaching their target hatch now. A thought struck her.

"Javier, why are we coming in from the side, rather than taking hatch number one on the centerline?" she asked.

"An oblique approach," he replied without explanation.

But she'd spent enough time around the man, and Djamila, to understand what they meant by that.

Come up on a problem from a side angle, rather than head on. Always being sneaky, as it were.

Afia approached the hatch and was able to free it quickly. Bethany waited on this side as the first four airlocked through, then she and Nikos joined them a few minutes later.

Djamila only had one pistol out, but that meant she was more keyed up for violence, not less. She had a hand free to strike anything that got close before she had time to shoot it. Hajna had her pistol out as well.

Bethany had one, holstered, just like Javier. It would remain there until she needed it.

Hopefully, hell would freeze over first.

Unlike the arboretum, the hallway was dark. Helmet lights cut it. They also revealed the dust in the air, even worse here than it had been aft.

"Why is it so murky?" Nikos asked.

"We're closer to life support," Afia replied. "Filters full of crap until we clean them, but the ship is not circulating much right now, so it stays up here. Probably worst at the first register."

"Where will that be?" Bethany asked, curious.

Naval architecture was not her forte.

"I'm guessing starboard and port," Javier said, pointing a little forward down the hallway. "About this far back from the bow on either side, with crew quarters and most living spaces between them on the bow. Or at least the important and beautiful people."

She grunted. That made sense, weird as it was.

The corridor still felt like she was walking in a fog.

"Hey folks, stand by," Afia announced. "Going to try something."

Bethany turned to see her kneeling next to the airlock controls. She had the panel itself off and was doing something to the wiring normally concealed behind it.

Suddenly, the hallway lit up. Some. About halfway. A foggy Monday morning in the fall as you were crossing the quad on the way to the library.

Visibility about ten meters. Bad for motor vehicles. Okay when walking, as long as nobody was jogging too fast and not paying attention.

"Good as we're going to get, I think," Afia said. "At least until I can get a crew in here to replace dead emitters."

Bethany nodded. All ships suffered wear and tear in space. Most of the crew spent much of their time fixing things as they broke down.

Part of the reason navies were so expensive to operate. Part of the reason she'd found herself unemployed. Until Javier came along and rescued her.

Still, the fog around her felt like morning. Spring, though, rather than fall.

This unbloomed rose found herself looking forward to it.

PART SIX

Suvi understood that survey was a state of mind. Patience, carved into seventy-three-meter-tall letters in the side of a mountain with a hammer and chisel. She was pretty good at it, too. Came of a form of immortality, mixed with hyper-fast processors, compared to humans, and the right programming.

She'd written a couple of symphonies while she'd been flying her patrols routes outside, but had first had to invent a couple of the instruments she needed. Nothing flew around here to bother her, so she'd been safe enough.

Now, they were inside the belly of the beast, so to speak. Good thing she had better sensors than humans did.

"Stand by," she announced. "I wanna try a thing."

Famous last words, but Javier had encouraged her from a young age to get silly.

Well, younger. She was way older than anybody else here, but she didn't say that.

Suvi was flying a drone designed for planetary surfaces in shitty weather. And Javier understood that.

She pinged the hallway with an ultrasonic pulse. The

kind guaranteed to piss off bats who were trying to sleep. The crap in the air was yuck, but she could work through it, just not as far as clean air. Still, it worked.

"Okay, everybody," she continued. "Adding a map on your right-hand panels on you heads-up-display."

She did. Showing her six organic friends this hallway and everything that beeping every third of a second could update.

Because Djamila, she added a real-time, hyperrealistic map overlay showing the Dragoon whatever her helmet saw. The lag was about a tenth of a second, so just enough to be detected.

"Excellent," Djamila announced. "Thank you."

Suvi could really only keep two of these going, and figured the big woman was the best candidate for the other one.

"Moving forward now," Suvi said.

The hallway was just a thing, but she didn't have to wade through a couple centimeters of yuck accumulated on the floor, either. That was their problem.

"Do we care about any doors?" she asked the group, using her laser to map the numbers on each one.

None had names right now, but Javier had said he expected them to be crew quarters up here. They were close enough to each other for that, each about three meters apart. If they ran the depth, you might have a long room, but she assumed that they had missed a corridor to another ring farther out. Most likely midship.

Nope, there was one, just coming into scanner range through the gunk fog.

"Heads up," she called now. "Radial corridor on the right."

"Javier?" Djamila asked over the main line.

"Don't ask me why, but that feels like the demarcation into officer country," he replied quietly.

"Third deck?" Bethany asked, reminding everyone that there were six here.

"Main deck is probably all botanical and zoological labs," he said. "Plus the bow comes up. Not much, but probably enough. Second deck would be offices, with storage aft on two and three. This feels like the center of the ship socially and emotionally. Six will also pinch down. I'd want a two or three deck vaulted ceiling with a transparent window forward to watch the stars, if I was building something this big and this silly."

"What would you build, Javier?" Nikos asked now, mostly silent until now.

Javier stopped walking, so Suvi held here, turret deployed to cover any monsters suddenly jumping out. Or even mice.

Never trust a mouse on a spaceship, either.

"I promised to take you back to *Ormint*, Nikos," Javier finally replied after a few seconds of thought. "Else I'd show you *Shangdu*, sometime."

"*Shangdu?*" the man asked. "Kublai Khan's reputed pleasure dome on the north China plains?"

"No," Javier shook his head. "The Khatum of *Altai*, one of our business partners, has a ship similar to this one. Two and a half kilometers long. One point three wide. It has a lake in the center that is an ellipse two kilometers long and one wide, so it takes up most of the ship by volume and mass. You can do that when you have the kind of wealth available that she has."

"I see," Nikos replied.

"Me, I'd build a plant ark," Javier said. "Noah style, but not animals. The old colony at *Svalbard*, where they have a seed vault against the ages, is a good start, but that's just things stored against emergencies later. I'd keep finding worlds that were previously terraformed by the machines and see what they were missing today."

"Missing?"

"Every terraforming includes all manner of plants," Javier continued. "The machines usually went back later to add animals, but not every environment is conducive. After this long, you start speciating again."

"So we should be dropping you and Rainier's dreamberry seed bombs from orbit?" Djamila asked.

Suvi was monitoring vital signs, so she registered the flush of heat indicating Javier's blush. Even if nobody else could see it.

"Maybe," he offered. "Wouldn't hurt anybody. And turns into another form of immortality for this crew."

Suvi liked the way he mentioned everybody, instead of just himself for having bred them, or Rainier St. Kitts for her work.

Everybody.

He started moving before anybody reacted, so Suvi spun her lifters into motion and led.

"Suvi, take the corner," he said firmly, so she did.

Another three-by-three corridor. This one let her map the interior volumes, since she had the exterior already and the arboretum.

"Estimated crew approximately three thousand," she announced generally, just to break up the awkward silence. "If we're crossing cabins, each person got an interior space roughly three meters wide by six deep. Cozy, but I assume either single-person or bunk beds."

"Agreed," Javier said. "You'd need strict population controls on things. I would presume that once you hit stability, you would have larger cabins for families, maybe knocking out the middle wall. I'd generally want a lot of common spaces, so folks were around people instead of brooding alone somewhere."

She could see that. Humans got weird when you left

them to their own devices for too long. She'd been programmed in an entirely different manner.

Patience. Letters carved seventy-three meters tall.

This corridor ran back thirteen meters, which seemed to break the pattern of threes, but then she thought about it and assumed a meter in between rooms for ducts and crawlspace. Power, water, air, whatever.

Djamila was next to Javier. Afia and Bethany after that. Nikos was moving in a state of euphoria, but she'd been pinging Hajna and the others to keep an eye on him. Not risky, just kid in a candy store kind of thing.

She could appreciate it. Not that she wanted to move out of *Excalibur*, but every ship grows old occasionally, and she'd need to live somewhere else at some point. Assuming the laws didn't change and nobody swore out a warrant for her arrest.

Best not to push it.

The radial intercepted a lateral corridor. Another ring.

Suvi turned and woke up any bats aft. Nobody phoned management or called the cops on her, so she presumed they were safe enough. Still, she always had pings that direction that could see a greater distance than Hajna could.

"Bow," Javier said when everyone caught up, so Suvi turned her drone's sprit into the wind, as it were. This ring was parallel to the inner one and the arboretum, even as the egg came to a point, so she assumed Javier was right about a forward lounge with a killer view. Assuming a space, it would be pretty good.

As always, she was scanning every placard and nameplate with her laser.

"Javier, you've got a life support machine on your left," she said, reading the ancient lettering almost faded to nothing now. "Maybe a control unit or something."

"Afia?" he asked.

The engineer moved up and did her breaking and entering magic now, popping a control panel off and poking at some wires. The door slid open about halfway and then hung.

The room practically exploded, except it was more of a bulge. Solid yuck, like you might stuff in a pillowcase if it was down instead of whatever crap had built up on any air filters.

Afia had jumped back. Everyone had jumped some.

Javier laughed.

"Gonna need Ilan's robot," he said, reaching out a hand and keying the door as closed as it would go.

Some of the gunk landed on the outside. She scanned it closer. Biological material.

Yuck.

Dead skin cells and whatever. Better to not think about it.

"Forward," Javier said. "We're close now."

Close to what? she wanted to ask. At the same time, so little was actually a surprise to her, considering the scanning power this platform had. She decided to let things unfold.

As long as no bats came to see who had woken them up.

PART SEVEN

J avier could feel it in his bones. Afia was the one supposedly blessed or cursed with the Second Sight by her grandmother, but Javier was back on the deck of *Hammerfield*, chasing ghosts.

Personally, he was surprised that nobody else had caught on to the possibilities. Maybe they'd all assumed everyone had left and gone to *Trotau Skale*, but he wasn't so sure.

"We should be about thirty meters?" he asked the armed lunatic flying in front of him, wondering how many arms she had right now and what silly outfit she'd dreamed up to wear today.

"To the centerline?" she replied. "Thirty-four at present."

"Look for a starboard-side door six meters back," he told her.

That felt right. Everything in three-meter chunks. He glanced over at Djamila, then back at the others, all trailing in general silence, like this was holy ground.

Wasn't, but he didn't want them putting too much thought into it.

"Nikos, how are you doing?" he asked, just to break people out of their shells right now.

"I'm fine, Javier," the scholar replied. "A bit overwhelmed."

"Been there," Javier replied with a smile in his voice. "Stellar archaeology expeditions are always a little weird, because so much culture gets wrapped up in the way you build a ship. Then it changes and jars you sideways."

"What does *Kimmeria* tell you?" the man asked.

"Old," Javier said. "Built the way they did during the Resource Wars, before piracy was really a thing between ships. You'd have landers and such for dropping down on a colony to steal everything on the ground."

"Or kill them and steal the claim," Djamila spoke up.

"Yeah, or that," he agreed. "Plus, the hardware for just about everything is two or three times the size of equivalent stuff today. Part of that was the General War, when everybody put so much money into pushing their tech so far so fast. We could do a lot of this on a smaller footprint, but they wanted something grand and imposing."

"That, they did," Nikos said. "What will we find at the bow?"

Javier stopped and considered it for a second.

"Could be anything," he temporized.

Without true cultural notes, he was only guessing at this point. Studies of humans and how they assembled themselves into groups.

At the micro, he would have compared it to reading a room. Javier supposed that it wasn't that different at the macro, at the end of the day.

"Pyramids, Nikos," he finally continued.

"Pyramids, Javier?"

"I think that the last few dead leaders will be waiting for us there," he said. "They abandoned the place, and then didn't come back for a long time. Went to *Trotau Skale*. What would you leave behind?"

"Dead kings in their mighty tombs?"

"That's what it feels like to me, Nikos."

"Then it is a good thing I only write ghost stories, and do not believe in them," the scholar laughed.

The others laughed as well, but it was a brittle sound. Not that it surprised him. Most people didn't like walking around on abandoned ships, unless they were in the process of cutting them apart to steal equipment.

Too superstitious, like Del.

"I've located your door, Javier," Suvi chimed in now. "Right where you expected it."

He nodded. Reading a room turned into reading a culture.

"Afia, assuming that it might be locked and don't freak out if it is," he explained. "There are other ways in."

"Anything you wanted to share?" she asked as they approached the portal.

"This was the social and emotional core of the vessel," he said. "The arboretum was where they had trees and critters for research and to have greenery around. This is where they came to drink off duty. I'm willing to bet you money that the bridge is on Deck Five, directly above us, with a vaulted ceiling in between."

"No bet," she replied instantly.

But she played poker with him and the pathfinders frequently.

Suvi, Djamila, and Hajna rearranged themselves with the noncombatants in the center as Afia went to work. The air was really bad here, but that made sense. Ilan's robots could clean the filters and dump everything into bags that would just get jettisoned into space.

Afia cursed and muttered as she worked. He grinned,

willing to bet on her and not whoever had decided to keep her out. Eventually, she would win, even if that involved going back to the ship for a cutting laser rated to *Excalibur*'s hull, which was thicker and tougher than this one.

Finally, she banged on something with a hand, and the goop she'd put into the tracks loosened it all. The hatch slid aftwards and the air poofed some into the forward compartment.

"Suvi?" he asked, not bothering to move.

Like Djamila would let him be first into a locked room. Especially this one.

"Oh, wow," Suvi said from inside. "Scanning."

He waited.

"Room is safe for entry," Suvi pronounced.

Javier was first in. Because, damn it, he would be.

Shit.

They'd turned off the life-support in here. Closed up the vents, even. He was letting some crap in due to the difference in air pressure; he could close the door shortly, once everyone was in.

In fact, that sounded good.

"Hajna, sorry, but you get to stay outside in case the door sticks," he said. "Everyone else in and close the door."

They did. He did.

Javier turned and looked over what might be his favorite tiki bar in the galaxy. Honest to goddess they had gone South Seas in here. Palm trees, but fake. Fronts made from something non-organic to still be hanging over a bar made of metal and painted like wood, or the metal chairs.

You wouldn't have wood, even with the arboretum. That was a museum. This was a bar.

Big bar between the two hatches, right on the centerline. Clear window across nearly thirty meters of bow, curved some with the hull and six meters tall.

Damned impressive.

"Javier, you need to see this," Suvi announced.

She was up. The vault in here was two full decks, so she was eight meters off the deck now, with a scanning laser painting a couple of boxes laid out right in front of that big window. Perpendicular to the front window, but touching.

He walked that way, the others trailing in his wake.

"Is that…?" Bethany asked before her voice caught hard in her throat.

Javier studied them. Four such boxes once he got close. Plexiglass or something. Transparent, but that just made it obvious as to what they were.

Coffins. Four of them.

Occupied.

"There are your kings," Javier told them.

BURIED TREASURE

PART ONE

Ilan studied the screen. Javier and Afia had both insisted that he seal engineering in, so everything was being done via short-range radio, powerful enough to overcome radiation leakage and hull walls.

Everyone except his immediate team was forward right now, exploring the four dead people and crap, but he still had a job to do. Not like three dead guys and one woman were going anywhere, either. Someone had sealed them in their coffins after embalming them or something, then pumped pure nitrogen in and welded everything.

Didn't look quite as good as the day they died, but not more than a year in the ground in a coffin, to look at them today.

He had other issues to deal with.

Afia and Javier lurking nearby didn't help, but at least they'd shut up, the third time he'd snapped at them.

Screen. Control sticks. Sensors. Status gauges. It was all there, like it had been that morning when he woke up, the image fully formed in his dream.

Suvi was in the room as a spare pair of eyes, but her

drone only had one waldo arm on it. Useful if something little happened, but not much since the robot outweighed her by a factor of about two hundred.

"Rolling forward on treads," he announced, mostly so people would stop breathing on his neck to offer advice. "Suvi, stand by."

She was pinging the hell out of the dead reactor, using more scanners that Ilan had realized Javier had built into that drone. Or maybe the Khatum's folks had snuck in a new platform and ported her over when nobody was looking. Creator knew Ilan had been busy with Afia and Andreea down in engineering, getting the big ship up to modern shipyard specs.

Suvi's light went green and blinked twice. Good enough.

The reactor had been at baseload. Javier and the others had gone up to Five and found the bridge of this beast. If you could call it that. Looked more like an insurance company office than anything. He supposed that living on *Storm Gauntlet* and then *Excalibur* had kinda warped his idea of what a bridge should look like, though.

Engineering was engineering. Reminded him more of Wilhelmina's ship. Lots of huge and inefficient power reactors, which made sense. You pointed the ship in a direction and just sailed inertially, hopping from time to time and maybe or maybe not plunking down into orbit to chat. Flight decks aft, above him right now, had once held a lot of shuttles, but all were long since gone, except one carcass that had been cannibalized for parts.

Probably not worth fixing at this point. Ugly box rather than something a collector might want.

His target reactor had suffered a failure sixteen years ago per the automated logs, which was damned impressive design work, since the other eleven were still operational. The ship would bring one on line each year, leave it quietly baseloading for three, then power it down and bring the next one up.

Except this one had gone boom. He'd need to see the blackbox, assuming it existed, to know why, but at least the breach had been polite.

"Approaching the gap," he said, watching as his three periscopes were synthesized into a single image. Like hunters with forward eyes, except he had three dimensions to work with.

Funky, but functional.

"Suvi, I am reading no change in radiation as I approach," Ilan said into the microphone. "Please confirm."

"Affirmative, Ilan," she said a moment later. "Looks like the room has stabilized."

Excellent.

"Translate that, kid?" Javier said. Except that he was standing clear across the hallway now. Only Afia was close.

"Thing blew seals during the incident," he replied, looking back. "Sprayed pressurized coolant everywhere before it shut down, but the machine is no longer really leaking. That means we can seal it here and wash everything down with something caustic enough to strip the surface level of metal or enamel, and maybe be back down to background counts when it dries."

"Who are you and what have you done with that clumsy punk?" Javier asked with a grin.

Ilan smiled and started to say something, but stopped.

"*Ugen*," he replied quietly instead, voice hoarse with emotions.

Everybody sobered at that. But it was the honest truth. Kid who'd climbed into that diving suit had never returned. Some other sea monster had emerged eight hours later.

Javier nodded.

Ilan took a deep breath and focused on his screen. He

pressed a button and a gigantic syringe needle came into his targeting reticle.

The reactor in front of him was not a standard design in any databank he could locate. Ms. Durbin, the Librarian, had already cursed up a storm and demanded that Javier take them on to Sector Prime, closest to *Earth* and containing the oldest colonies, so she could buy, copy, or steal old engineering specs.

Like the woman already knew they'd do crap like this more than once in the future.

Not that Ilan was arguing with her.

But volume was volume. Half-lives were predictable, so he knew how much material had been inside the thing on day one. That meant he could calculate exactly how much internal volume there should be.

"Stand by for sealant," he said, mostly to Suvi, so she could watch in case what he was doing blew out somewhere else. Or he had more leaks than he knew about.

The robot had twice as much material as he needed. Javier had taught him that trick.

Now the fiddly part. He locked the treads in place and extended the syringe like a giant scorpion, delicately shifting it around until he was pretty sure.

"Suvi, confirm insertion," Ilan said.

"Depth about four centimeters," she replied. "Can you go any deeper?"

He tried, but stopped only one more centimeter inside.

"Touching something inside," Ilan said. "Backing out a little and deploying."

Two quick flicks and he opened the rocker control over the pump. Took a deep breath.

"You got this," Afia said from close by.

Nerves. Nothing more than that.

Ilan Yu had invented a new thing. A kind of maintenance

robot he could use for all sorts of places that humans shouldn't go.

Assuming, like Ms. Durbin did, that they'd end up doing crazy shit like this again.

He pushed the button and listened as audio sensors told him the pumps in there were running. Hydraulics would push until he stopped them, or pressure got too high because it was full.

He switched to Suvi's optics now, since his were too close and right up against the reactor vessel.

"Got a small leak, bottom right," she informed him.

Ilan looked but it seemed safe. And the stuff would react to air, lack of pressure, and heat to harden, so hopefully it would seal itself in. That had been the goal. Just keep the radioactive fuel contained and then they could cut out this reactor if they had to.

The aft hull was touching the back of the beast. Six quick cuts and he could vent the engineering space to pull the carcass out. Doing that, however, would be an admission of defeat on his part.

Screw that. Gonna entomb you in place, until I can take apart one of the others and figure out how to fix you. Or build a replacement from scratch, because you people were space barbarians compared to us modern folk.

He didn't say that out loud, though. And Javier and others had teased him enough that he didn't mutter under his breath when he worked anymore. Much.

Instead, he watched the pressure gauge as the semi-fluid went in.

"Think I'm close," he said. "Stopping the pumps. Suvi, it should take thirty seconds, then be hard to the touch of your waldo. I'll back out shortly and you swap me places."

"Roger that," she said.

He flipped the rocker closed and withdrew his stinger.

No fluid jetted out, so hopefully he was good. Just kind of oozed, so maybe he'd nailed it just right to fill the interior with a new coolant that would harden in place and he'd been dead on about the volume.

"Engines reversing," he said, backing the robot out of the space and moving closer to the door.

Like everything in there, he'd have to wash the robot down, back in a decontamination bay on *Excalibur*. Good thing he'd built a big enough tent.

On his screen, Suvi moved over and extended her waldo, tapping on the side of the reactor vessel.

"Yeah, I think that did it," she announced after a few seconds. "Radiation is down a little from predictions, so maybe we've sealed things tight."

Afia leaned over and planted a kiss on the top of his head. The Dragoon was there as well with a hand on his shoulder.

Ilan accepted all the congratulations and smiled. Just doing his job.

"ALERT!" Suvi suddenly called on all channels.

It took Ilan a second to realize that it was on the ship channel and not the one he'd been talking to the drone on. Different Suvi.

Maybe *Main* Suvi.

"All hands to combat stations," this new Suvi announced. "Stand by for enemy warships."

Ilan started to stand up, but Javier waved him back.

"You fix things here," the Science Officer said. "The drone can always rescue you if you have to abandon. Everyone else forward to the camp while we sort this out."

Ilan nodded and went to work again. He had an entire checklist to complete.

Even in the middle of a battle.

PART TWO

K iliyn kept his snarl off his face.
Barely.

"What do you mean, we're too late?" he asked in as polite of a voice as he might be able to manage at this moment.

Captain Avison actually took a step back, even on her own bridge, surrounded by her crew. But the woman was only a pirate by association. Nobody wore pistols or cutlasses around here. Mostly just doing jobs on a spaceship.

One that happened to occasionally work outside the law.

"We picked up a visual signal and moved closer to investigate it," she reminded him now.

Behind her, Milya stood poised, but unmoving.

His mission. Supposedly.

His failure, right this second.

"And?" Kiliyn asked when the captain paused.

"And *Excalibur* is sitting right next to it," Avison said. "They are scanning nearby space and transmitting an identification transponder. This one also translates with an additional flag of *Diver Down*."

"What does that mean?" Milya asked now, interrupting

227

and moving around to the third point of a triangle with him and the captain. The crew glanced up, but nobody made any hostile moves.

Not even Kiliyn. He had already failed. Violence wasn't going to solve anything at this moment.

"It means that they have crews aboard the wreck," Avison said. "Exploring or salvaging. We won't know until we're much closer."

"Have they seen us?" Kiliyn asked now.

"Not yet," Avison said. He could see the caginess in her eyes now. "We came out a ways from the ship, and their scanners won't report us as another ship at this range since we're running quiet. At least I think not."

"I would be willing to bet that you were wrong about that, Captain Avison," Kiliyn replied, grimacing. "Knowing how well armed that ship should be, can we approach to a safe distance to communicate with them?"

"They have enormous Pulsars from what you've told me and what I know of the class," Avison replied. "Turrets on all sides, plus Pulse Cannons and torpedoes. We can stay back and program an emergency jump. Probably about a quarter of a second of lag, assuming they don't immediately move to attack us."

Kiliyn considered it. She had warned him that *Adamant Capital* was a mere corsair. Something that formal navies might have called a patrol destroyer. *Excalibur* rated as an enforcer by their standards. A cruiser capable of crushing the smaller ship in a direct encounter.

He had no choice.

"Jump us closer, Captain," he said now, taking a deep breath. "Not close enough to put us at risk, but close enough to talk."

She studied his face for a moment, seeking some clue.

Perhaps she even found it, because Captain Avison nodded to herself and turned to the rest of the bridge.

"All hands to battle stations," she said calmly. "Everyone into emergency suits. That's you two as well. Stand by for a jump."

Kiliyn moved to where his and Milya's suits were normally stored, a locker off to one side.

As they began pulling everything out to put on, she murmured quietly for his ears alone.

"Are you certain this is wise?" she asked.

"No," Kiliyn replied. "What choice do I have?"

PART THREE

Suvi had been doing twenty-three things at once, like normal. Girl had those kinds of options with this grade of hardware.

She had detected the first ripples of an emerging ship as soon as space/time began to wobble. Both Javier and Zakhar had made it a point to leave the overlocks disabled, especially after *Nidavellir*, so she spun all weapons in that direction as quickly as she could start bringing generators on line. Shields came up glacially slow, but that was her thinking at her optimal combat speed.

To a human, it was less than an eyeblink.

Suvi aimed **ALL** of her eyes at the intrusion and pinged it hard enough that any bats on *Kimmeria* would be awake in about two seconds.

And locked every weapon with arc on it. The rest went into combat overwatch, just in case some silly hooligan had thought to hop a sacrificial lamb in on her first, then drop a Warmaster on a blind side.

Weren't no blind sides on this ship.

"ALERT!" Suvi called on all channels, local intercom as well as the radios to her forward crews over on the wreck.

Just because, she also tuned all of her science shards down a few notches. Every bit of multiplexing she could eke out now might be the difference. In her mind, she was back at *Nidavellir* and about to face off with that silly Warmaster *Meridian*.

"All hands to combat stations," she followed up a second later. "Stand by for enemy warships."

One of the many reasons she loved Zakhar Sokolov was that he didn't immediately start issuing silly or contrary orders even before he knew what the hell was going on.

"Suvi, do I have time to get to the bridge?" he asked instead, currently forward getting some coffee in the lounge.

"Affirmative, sir," she replied, back in the *Concord* Navy as a bad-ass probe-cutter Yeoman going into dangerous places. The good old days. "Piet has the bridge at present."

"Roust everyone anyway," he said, grabbing his empty mug and headed aft.

She made a note to have someone deliver a carafe in a few minutes. Maybe ask Collette or Simone, down in *Le Bistrot Parisien* to brew up a pot of really chewy stuff they way like they liked it. Someone finding her out here was up to some form of no good.

Wasn't a dark alley scenario. Or if it was, this girl could take care of herself.

It was the muggers who might need rescuing shortly.

PART FOUR

J avier kept the profanities to himself. He didn't figure he'd screwed up that bad. Most likely, Brinov and his girlfriend had finally caught up. Faster than Javier had expected, but unless they brought a really big hammer with them, he was still in charge.

Worse, his girl was sitting over there like a mother hen.

Y'all best be polite.

He was running. Djamila was even being polite today and merely jogging along so he could keep up. Afia's legs were whirling like a cartoon. Forward and around the ring.

Nothing around here flew, so he didn't see any of the critters down there in the arboretum. Most of them were shy anyway, living quiet lives in their little forest since there was no cover once you moved away from the center of that bowl.

"Del, are you listening?" Javier managed as he ran.

"Oh, yeah," the old man said quickly. "This is all a conspiracy to make me land on that damned ghost ship, isn't it?"

"I doubt it," Javier replied. "Bad practical joke to play on folks if it is. Not that I'd put it past Zakhar, but Suvi wouldn't go all in like this. Feels like a real drop."

"Where do you want me?" Del asked.

That, right there, was why Javier was willing to put up with all the other crap Delridge Smith brought to the table on a daily basis. Shit was about to go down, and he fell into line with everyone else, instead of turning into yet another wild card.

"Figure out what we're facing first," Javier decided. "If they are big and close, get your ass inside the bay here to hide. If not, cross back over to *Excalibur* and board but stay hot in case you have to start flying rescue missions."

"On it," Del said. And he was gone.

Javier noted the way the gun bunnies were on alert, but not slacking on their usual duties. Helped that they were all ground troops with nothing to do if a space battle broke out.

Except prepare to board an enemy vessel and shoot people.

He doubted that would be necessary.

No. Wrong word.

Hoped.

Brinov and Kuzmandieva hadn't been bad guests. Pretty nice people, just a little stuffy and weird, but he put that down to the planet they came from. Weird place.

They'd just brought help.

"Suvi, we're at base camp," he said as everyone staggered to a halt.

Six years ago, he'd have been blowing like a badly tuned combustion engine right now, but Djamila and Emma St. Kitts had everyone in way better shape. Not running laps around *Excalibur* in heavy packs like Sykora and her people, but capable of that quick burst.

"What are we facing?" Javier asked.

"Corsair-scale vessel just popped out of jump," Suvi

replied instantly. "Transponder *Adamant Capital*. Nobody I know. Light-speed lag of about .22 seconds. They are cleared for action, but can't hit me worth a damn at this range. They just want to talk?"

"That's my guess," Javier said. "Zakhar doing anything?"

"I am watching patiently, Javier," the man joined them now. "Stand by a moment."

Javier counted noses. Nikos was back safe on the ship. Sascha and Hajna were forward with a group cataloging artifacts and trying to identify them while under strict instructions not to touch anything dangerous.

Whatever that meant.

He had Djamila and Afia with him. Everyone else were just crew with regular jobs.

"Attention unknown vessel," Zakhar came over the line in that big, booming, Captain-of-Doom voice he did when you pissed the man off. Like now. "We are currently undertaking a salvage exploration with crews in the wreckage. If you make any hostile moves, I will annihilate you. If you fire on anything I can scan, I will make it a point to hunt down every escape pod you launch after your ship is destroyed, and finish them off as well. I hope I am clear on that point and you wish to behave like civilized beings today. Reply on this channel."

Javier grinned.

That little Frigate *Ajax*, back at *Nidavellir*, had gotten the sharp end of things when they'd fired that shot that nearly killed Afia, but for Ilan's quick thinking.

"*Excalibur*, this is Captain London Avison, aboard *Adamant Capital*," a woman's voice came through now. "I have someone who wants to talk to you. And yes, we are just here to talk."

"Captain Sokolov, this is Kiliyn Brinov," the man said now. "I'd like to talk about the ship."

Javier nodded. He keyed a private channel to the bridge.

"Zakhar, why don't we invite him over to the wreck?" Javier said. "Milya and a couple of folks from the ship can come with him. Del can go pick them up. Assuming you don't have a need to carry through your threats."

"As long as he behaves," Zakhar replied. "You sure about that? Could be a trap."

"I have Djamila and all her people over here, Zakhar," Javier laughed. "And Suvi in her combat drone. Unless they are bringing an entire army, I'm not worried. Not even really worried then."

"Fine, you invite him," Zakhar said.

Javier switched back to the main channel now.

"Kiliyn, this is Javier," he said. "If you'd like to join us on *Kimmeria*, you'll need skinsuits or something tougher. Our pilot can come over and grab a half dozen folks for a tour. Then we can talk about what happens next."

Long pause. Silly boy probably had expected Javier to be all bluster and threat, like Zakhar. Bad Cop/Worse Cop, maybe.

But there was space in the galaxy for good cops, too. As long as everyone behaved.

"What are you doing to the ship, Javier?" the man asked now.

"Right now, I have a team repairing a failed generator aft," Javier said. "Another team is cataloging things forward. Haven't yet figured out how to handle the zoological issues."

"Zoolo…?"

"There's an atmosphere in here, Kiliyn," Javier replied. "Small animals and trees have survived, though things are not safe for you or me. Plus, as soon as we try to fix anything, we might kill them and I'd rather not. My experts tell me they might have evolved into new species now."

Longer pause.

Fool forgot that he was dealing with a man who had once had *THE SCIENCE OFFICER* etched into a mug so that the boardroom pixies had a harder time denying that they knew who it belonged to.

Didn't stop them. Just made them come up with more creative excuses for stealing his coffee.

More than once, Javier had considered building Suvi a flying tanker drone that could dock with a coffee maker and then deliver the stuff fresh, wherever he was.

Of course, if he did that, Javier had no doubts someone would invent a game of air piracy with small drones to try to hijack his coffee. He had a good crew, in spite of them all being treacherous slime turds some days.

"I'd like to see that," Kiliyn said now in a quiet, hushed tone that Javier understood.

He'd been the same way when he'd realized that there was atmosphere in here. And life.

"Del, you on line?" Javier asked.

"Am."

"Can you grab the Doctors St. Kitts and bring them with you?" he said. "And Nikos and Leonora? This sounds like time to convene a scientific conference, and this is as good a place as any."

"Will do."

The line went silent, but Javier wasn't fooled. Del was having a terrible crisis now. Did he land, or make them jump? Did he join them and see the inside of the ship that everyone had been talking about, or just play the gruff tough guy, too stubborn to be impressed by anything?

Javier switched to the inside comm.

"Ilan and Suvi, what's your status aft?" he asked.

"Ready whenever you want to pressurize Engineering and see what else needs to be repaired," Ilan replied. "Still have to hose everything down, but I can build you the machines for that and Suvi can fly them."

"Good," Javier said. "I'll need both of you forward in about an hour. Your team can handle babysitting things aft for a while."

"Roger that."

He turned to Djamila. Grinned up at her.

"You're in charge of security," he said.

"Yes."

Nothing more. Wasn't even a question. Her, Sascha, and Hajna. Iqbal and his goofs. Suvi in the armed drone. He was not worried.

"Javier, should I remain here?" Zakhar said.

"Yeah, I think so," Javier replied. "Plausible deniability later, or something. Plus, you might need to carry out your threat if anyone gets stupid. Make sure you avenge me well."

"I'll immortalize you, ya silly punk," the man said.

Javier laughed. He had no doubts that this would contribute mightily to whatever legend he was accumulating.

But everything didn't have to be filtered through the lens of that killer, Eutrupio Navarre.

Javier Eutropio Aritza could do things, too.

PART FIVE

Bethany often felt like a fifth wheel with the crew of *Excalibur*. An extra piece that really didn't have a place with the misfits and former pirates.

Until today.

Javier had sent her forward with a few folks to catalog things that they'd found in the lounge. The bodies were still there. Three men and a woman, dead for however long, save that someone had entombed them aboard *Kimmeria* and then left in the last shuttle. Possibly that same empty bay that had become her home away from home here.

The alert had jarred her hard into her past, but Javier had ordered her to keep at her task. To date, nothing they'd found in the last several days had contained any magical properties or *unobtanium* materials like you always found in stories of lost civilizations. Just the detritus of lives lost.

She had told everyone to take the rest of the day off and folks had returned with her to the inner base camp with a view of the forest down in the bowl. Occasionally, she wondered if the creatures down there might mistake the humans for long-lost gods, returned to disrupt everything with new theologies.

Possibly not the furthest from the truth, at the end of the day.

Her people settled, Bethany was standing somewhat behind Javier now. The camp looked like something of a picnic in a metal park, with the addition of two semi-rigid tents where folks could step into a shower unit to wash off the gunk and radiation from their suits before emerging on the inside to strip and relax in shirt sleeves. Or at least pop off their helmet and eat.

Just about everything else could be done in the suit, including recharging power, adding fresh oxygen, and refilling her canteen bladder.

She'd been living in the suit now for long enough that Bethany was almost feeling like an expert.

She turned and looked around one last time. Afia and Ilan were flanking Javier. She was off in a corner, out of the way. The engineering team was still at their own end of the ship, hard at work.

Djamila and her crew, plus Suvi, were in the outer bay, keyed up for violence that Bethany didn't expect. Del had finally relented exactly enough to land his rear gear only on magnets, then open the bay, but not enough to come fully inside.

Adamant Capital had remained at a tremendous distance, where neither ship could threaten the other. Again, probably just as well.

"Everybody, stand by," Djamila came over the line now. "Triggering the inner airlock."

"Y'all have fun," Del said, so Bethany knew that he was in the process of getting back outside, where the walls wouldn't close in on him.

She didn't know what haunted the man. He always got

extremely polite and formal, any time it sounded like she might be prying into his past, so Bethany generally left him alone.

The beeps of the lock brought her attention.

Djamila emerged, followed by Sascha and the Doctors Askvig. All seemed to be smiling, so the flight over must not have been too stressful.

Kiliyn Brinov and Milya Kuzmandieva emerged next, followed by a thick woman of normal height. Captain London Avison, off *Adamant Capital*. Emma and Rainier followed them, and then all the rest of Djamila's team came through, Hajna and Helmfried first.

The visitors were unarmed, as demanded, but Javier had offered everyone a safe passage back in an hour.

Nikos walked right over and gave her a hug. Leonora surprised Bethany by doing the same. The two scholars ended up on either of her flanks in a manner similar to how Sascha and Hajna were standing just behind Djamila now. Or Afia and Ilan were with the Science Officer.

Rainier and Emma kind of drifted off to one side. Rainier had come over once, but Javier had been keeping everyone out of the forest, save for a few leaves and things Suvi had collected for the woman to examine.

Kiliyn and Milya came to rest in front of Javier. Captain Avison was off to their right, on Emma's side and away from Djamila.

"How did you find it?" Kiliyn asked in a voice that managed to split the difference between hostile and curious. "How did you even know it existed?"

"You were wearing a brooch at dinner one night," Javier explained now. "It has a diffraction grating etched inside that contains both a map and a set of identifying clues. When we hit *Ormint*, I dropped down to the surface and played a pretty random hunch that led me to Nikos."

"Yes, you managed to find him and leave the planet with the man even before I knew who he was, let alone talked to the man," Kiliyn replied.

Bethany found Javier's shrug instructive. He wasn't denying anything. But then, why should he? The laws of salvage were pretty well known, and the ship had been in space alone for a very long time.

"Dumb luck on my part," Javier said. "And a good team of people. Never discount that. I don't have to be perfect, if I'm lucky and got experts handy to ask."

"And the ship?"

"The map was pretty good," Javier shrugged again. Bethany noted that he didn't mention Suvi's part in all this, or her abilities. "How did you find us so quickly?"

"We had the original instructions on a map in my quarters," Kiliyn replied. "Written on paper, but I didn't think you had accessed it."

"We didn't," Javier said. "Got lucky on the math and only needed three jumps to get here. Then we boarded and have been exploring. Mostly empty rooms, because folks loaded up everything they could before they left."

"So all this was for nothing?" the man asked.

Bethany could hear the despair creep into his voice.

"Not at all," Javier derailed him. "Ilan here just finished plugging a radiation leak aft in engineering that had destroyed one of twelve reactors, but the others appear to be intact. It's what is forward that I wanted to show you. Bit of a walk, but the low gravity makes it a pleasant stroll. Care to join me?"

"What is it?" Kiliyn asked.

"Better if you see it with your own eyes first," Javier said. "Then we'll talk botany."

"Botany?"

Javier turned at that point, gesturing the newcomers to

join him as he walked out to the edge of the promenade and waved a hand at the trees, down in the bowl of Deck One in the middle distance. She heard the gasps.

"All this survived," Javier said. "But is extremely delicate right now. We haven't even started cleaning the air filters, because we're not sure what damage we might do, returning everything to the pristine environment. Or what creatures we might accidentally kill."

"Creatures?" Milya asked now.

"Suvi, could you project your tree-roos for me?" he asked.

Bethany watched a hologram come into existence on the waist-high wall that kept people from falling off this deck. *Earth*-like tree-kangaroo, but tiny. Possibly unique in the universe, though she and Suvi didn't have nearly the depth or breadth of encyclopedia to know for certain.

Yet…

Again, folks gasped and made strange noises. How often did you find a derelict in space that still had life on it, a thousand years later?

Like the tree-roos, this ship might be unique in the annals of human space exploration. That was a testament to how well the ancestors of the Avalon Project had built it, and the things they had achieved later.

"Bethany, could you tour guide us all forward now?" Javier asked. "Our guests need to know what we found."

She nodded. They did, except she wasn't sure what the implications of it would be. Or the outcome.

Javier Aritza held almost all the cards here, but the man played poker at a terribly high level, and was holding things close to the chest right now.

Bethany supposed that she would find out the truth at the same time everyone else did.

PART SIX

Kiliyn found himself holding Milya's hand as they walked. Weirdly, London took up his other hand, putting him in the middle. He didn't think that the woman was making a sexual statement, so much as perhaps seeking human touch in this ancient tomb that had held his ancestors. They were surrounded by strangers here.

London was completely the outsider here. He and Milya had at least traveled with Javier and the others from *Trotau Skale* to *Ormint* together.

Around them, the crew from *Excalibur* calmly—almost casually—followed Bethany Durbin and Javier forward, though Kiliyn kept finding his eyes drawn to that forest over there, sometimes imagining that he could see little animals moving about. Animals his great-great-however-great grandparents might have known.

How had it come to this? Would that truth ever be known?

They arrived at the center of the bow, where the egg shape came down to as much of a point as the ship knew. Again, they airlocked through, into a space where they were standing in almost a fog of gunk that he recognized from a life-support system that had not been cleaned.

In centuries.

And yet, they could not clean it now, possibly, without destroying the unique ecosystem that had evolved behind him.

Kiliyn turned to Rainier St. Kitts. He remembered the woman from the first trip.

"Doctor, how quickly would the animals have evolved?" he asked, watching others turn as well.

"Assuming they are similar to ancestral forms, we can estimate a generation of about ten years, as an average," she said. "Suvi has found no predatory forms, but we presume that they would begin to move that direction, perhaps turning into omnivores first. What nobody knows is how long the ship has been in the current state, versus what we presume it was like when abandoned. Do you know how long ago that was? We've only been able to estimate."

"*Kimmeria* departed from *Earth* in 5497," he told her. "It was our home until 6619, when those of us who survived moved to *Trotau Skale* and started over."

"So nine hundred and thirty-four years," she replied with a nod. "Ninety to one hundred generations. Enough time to speciate, perhaps. I'm a botanist, and those trees will live for centuries, so we can examine them and easily move the atmosphere back to something they could survive."

"But not the tree-kangaroo," he said.

"Perhaps not," she agreed. "That will require a great deal more study before we can even estimate. At present, all we have is a rough census showing around five hundred of the tree-kangaroos as well as smaller animals."

Kiliyn knew a different kind of failure now. Javier was not acting like a pirate set on sailing the ship into a yard and having it broken apart. Nor of turning it into some sort of bizarre zoo.

What was the man up to?

Kiliyn found himself completely lost, and his destiny was simply out of his hands.

"So we found the bridge of the vessel," Javier explained now as they came to rest in the hallway. "It is above us on Deck Five. This is Deck Three."

"What's on the other side of these doors, Javier?" Kiliyn asked nervously.

"What you came here to find, Brinov," the man replied.

He nodded to Durbin now and she palmed the door controls.

"Everyone in quickly so we don't introduce too much air pollution," Durbin said, gesturing folks to move.

Kiliyn hadn't been paying attention earlier, but the six armed men had stayed behind at the thing they called base camp. He was not, however, foolish enough to believe that he could somehow threaten Djamila Sykora. And Emma St. Kitts had taught classes in marital arts and yoga on his first voyage.

Perhaps London might manage to do something, but they were outnumbered. All Kiliyn had to go on was Javier's promise of safe passage.

Hopefully, it would be enough.

Then he saw the thing that Javier had found. As he had said, the reason that Kiliyn had come.

Four, clear coffins, just as the ancient stories had remembered them for eternity.

He turned to Javier, but words failed him.

PART SEVEN

Javier watched as the man had something of a religious experience. He himself didn't grok that sort of thing, himself. At the same time, he'd been raised with a firm and patient belief in the *Concord* and its **Navy** as the good guys in the universe.

That wasn't entirely wrong, much of the time, even though he had a much better grip of power politics today than he'd had when he wore the green professionally.

Javier nodded to the man and began to walk, the three strangers falling in behind him.

That same window into deep space that represented the bow of the ship. Four coffins left as they'd been found.

Most of this crew had been there when *Hammerfield* had been recovered, with her entire remaining crew dead in similar coffins. The newcomers would have quickly picked up the reverence for the dead from their seniors.

At least this solved the problem for Javier of what to do with the only four corpses buried here. He'd had weird visions of turning back to *Trotau Skale* and just delivering the

249

coffins with a cheery "*Hello, were you missing these?*" to those folks.

Minus lots of explanation.

Brinov could handle that task for now. However he thought appropriate.

"Do you know who they are?" he asked.

"We do not," Javier said quietly, watching how all the rest of the crew had fallen into something of a professional formation, a hemisphere surrounding him, Bethany, and the three outsiders. "I've found the ship's logs, but not really gone deep into things, as they were using a strange technology to record things. Archaic, because as near as I can tell it hasn't been used by the rest of the galaxy in a couple thousand years."

Brinov nodded and stepped close, studying them.

"You haven't opened the coffins?" he asked, surprised.

"Sealed in tight by professionals," Javier replied, rapping on the nearest one with his knuckles. "Filled with pure nitrogen according to my sensors, so pretty much unchanged since. I'm not above salvage, but interred bodies are a whole different matter. *Hammerfield* had her entire final crew aboard in similar boxes when we first boarded her to claim the ship. Plus, to us, they are just dead people. I'm sure at some point the logs would allow us to identify them, but we've been cataloging things first."

"Cataloging?" Milya asked now, stepping half a stride into his space to look up at him.

She looked different now than she had before. More assertive.

Javier wondered if she'd been the mastermind and Brinov just the pretty face on this one. He understood how that kind of grift was run.

"Bethany?" he asked, turning to his Librarian.

Her folks had been in here, like he'd expected, but the

room was huge and they'd gotten out of the way quickly, only to now fall into a second, formal line with the rest.

Formation, by a group of civilians.

Weird.

And appropriate.

Bethany turned to her right and gestured to a *thing*.

"Secondary operations console and environmental systems computer," she said, laying a hand atop the small box with various buttons, knobs, and screens. "Ambient music and atmosphere could be set for the room, depending on the mood. There is a similar one over in the area that we take to be a bar, even though it was stripped bare of everything except the shelves. Presumably hauled to the colony."

Javier watched Brinov and Milya follow her. London Avison wasn't a woman he knew, even by reputation, but Belfast didn't operate in the realms where Javier had spent the last twenty years.

Bethany took her time, even dragging a couple of her engineers into the spotlight to discuss some of the strange objects and systems that they had found.

All of it was ancient. He felt more like an archaeologist than anything.

Finally, they finished circling the grand lounge and ended up back at the coffins. In between, they'd seen electronics in the walls left in place. Communications and entertainment units too big or complicated perhaps for a small colony. Chairs not sturdy enough to survive a hard winter.

Those little bits of shit left over when you've taken everything you can pack, like an abandoned apartment when you've moved out.

"I can tell you one name for certain," Brinov said now. "Naida Bedova, the only female left behind. The other three are Zimir Lischko, Sergi Tapkima, and Laval Tenkiy, but I am not sure that we have any pictures of them after all this time. So much was lost, that first generation of struggle on *Trotau Skale.*"

"I can get you some," Suvi suddenly spoke up from her drone. "Having names means I can compare to records. Stand by."

Everyone spun around as she came over heads and pointed her marker laser at them.

"This is Laval," she said, moving to the next one. "Zimir. Sergi. I have that much of their security software unraveled to be able to match credentials with faces, once you gave me the names I needed to look for."

Brinov and Milya both gasped. Avison was made of tougher stuff. Or less emotionally involved. Not a lot of difference.

"So now what, Javier?" Brinov turned to face him.

Not confrontational, or Djamila might have bounced him off a bulkhead to teach him better manners. More like a man clutching at a rope in a storm that has washed him overboard.

"There was a specific reason I did this, Brinov," Javier said.

"Loot?"

"Far from it," Javier laughed. "There are any number of stories about flying Dutchmen out there. Old, forgotten ships that might be reclaimed, and with them all of their legends. Nikos and Leonora have been filling my crew's heads with such things. They'll do the same to you and your folk, given half a chance."

He liked the way the Askvigs jumped almost as much as the outsiders. Meant that nobody had seen what he was up to.

Useful, to keep folks on their toes.

"When this ship disappeared, it was filled with scientists,"

Javier continued. "Boffins intent on sailing forever into the darkness where the rest of human society wouldn't be able to bother them as they did whatever they thought appropriate."

"And?" Milya asked now.

"And my great concern was that they'd gone and invented some fantastically dangerous new technology that might represent a threat to that same galaxy that they had left behind," Javier said. "I don't trust people who decide to keep secrets at a cultural level. It is occasionally something embarrassing, but more frequently some manner of crime against civilization. That gets my hackles up."

"So you got here first?" Milya asked now.

"That's right," Javier nodded, not even the least bit intimidated or bothered to admit these things.

He had a warship handy, had it been necessary to blow this ship to hell. Or to stop Brinov from claiming it.

Didn't need to now.

"What did you find?" she asked. "You did not chase us off, nor demand that you got all the salvage."

"We found nothing," he said with a simply grin.

"Nothing?" she asked, crestfallen.

He watched her turn to take in the room, as well as the four elders.

"But…?"

"Oh, we found a lot of history here," Javier interrupted her before she could get wound up in herself. "Don't get me wrong there. But the ship itself is completely unarmed, which tells you just how old it had to have been. And the technology that we did find was pretty amazing and advanced in its day. However, that day was Late Resource Wars period. This stuff would have been bleeding edge tech until about the middle of the Corporate Wars Era, but by the time it was abandoned, the first of the Pocket Empires had been proclaimed and their tech had long since blown past the folks on *Kimmeria*."

"Really?" she asked.

"Ilan had just finished entombing the reactor that failed when you folks arrived," Javier nodded. "I asked him, because he's into that sort of thing, and those designs were so ancient he didn't know them. From the power load they put out, our own reactors these days would be at least a third smaller, maybe more because we haven't brought any of them above minimum to see how much they could output."

"Oh…"

"Same with the hull," Javier continued. "The metallurgy was fantastic for the day, and archaic now. The electronics. *Et cetera*. Everything about this ship did represent a tremendous leap forward technologically, but that was, as you've said, twenty-one hundred years ago. And a lot of wars, which tend to compress innovation. There's nothing at all like Suvi or her cousins about this ship. Just a significant automation suite that let it continue working this long when all the humans had left."

"You aren't claiming it?" Milya asked, dumbfounded.

"What would I do with it?" he asked, hands turned palm up. "Turn it into a museum and zoo? I'd have to spend a fortune and several years in the process, neither of which appeal to me. What I'd like to do is extract a promise from the three of you—and your superiors, Captain Avison—to do exactly that. *Ormint* would probably love to fund a project like that, because I doubt that *Trotau Skale* could afford it. You might, however, convince Nikos's university to let you put it at *Trotau Skale* in orbit and then charge tourists and scholars for access to see such an ancient past with their own eyes."

He really liked the looks of surprise that greeted him, from the outsiders as well as most of his own folks.

Most.

Bethany and Djamila were grinning at him. Suvi probably was as well. The others were still thinking like pirates.

More the fools them.

"I get the feeling that you're fine with just walking away at that point," Brinov said.

"You'll need years to solve the tree-roos," he countered. "Biologists will make their career on it and the other fauna around here. The rest of the ship is a pretty amusement park, as far as I'm concerned. Either I spend all my time keeping you people from destroying it for something that's just not there, or I trust you to take care of it and let you figure out how turn it into a money-making proposition. I have other horizons to explore, many light-years from here. Besides, I've already found the thing I was looking for."

"What was that?" Milya asked, as Brinov was just standing there mute, jaw hanging open.

"Friends," Javier grinned at the woman. "And buried treasure."

EPILOGUE

Javier wanted to be able to lean back and put his feet up on something. Maybe hook his hands behind his neck. Stretch out, as it were.

He settled for leaning back in his chair and crossing his ankles.

He was in Zakhar's office, with Djamila in the other seat and Bethany standing against the wall, arms crossed in a way that conveyed irritation rather than embarrassment.

Javier grinned at her. Zakhar was the only one in green today, but Bethany still managed to convey militant fierceness.

"And that's it?" Zakhar asked.

Javier shrugged.

"I still think we got the better end of the deal," he replied. "Short of trophies with sentimental value, there's nothing over there worth the effort."

"And letting Nikos and Leonora transfer to *Adamant Capital* instead of traveling with us?" Zakhar asked.

"Saves us the effort of returning to *Ormint*," Javier offered.

"How do you know they won't just cut the ship up and salvage it?" Bethany broke in now. "That's the part I haven't calculated."

Zakhar's laugh interrupted, so Javier nodded to the man.

"That's a rare enough alloy, sure," he began. "At the same time, we can make better. And have for a long time because somebody came up with a tougher formula. They'd have to melt it all down for raw stock and remix it. Lot of metal there, but not enough. Generators are in pretty good shape, per Ilan and Afia, but again, we build better now everywhere, so they have historic value and not much more."

"And we get nothing for our effort?" Bethany asked.

"We did copy the entire computer system," Djamila said. "Suvi is in the process of slowly reading and converting those files. Even at her speed, she estimates that it will take her better than half a year to complete."

"Update that to three and a half months," Suvi broke in from the wall monitor behind him. "I've found the key they use to separate personal journal files from automated diagnostics. Most of those I will be able to ignore until I run into some event that someone talks about, like a breakdown."

"Suvi, how long would it take Nikos to translate those logs, assuming he had the programming skills to write the kinds of tools he would need?" Javier asked, eyes still watching Bethany.

"Approximately eighteen years, assuming he worked at it eight hours per day and kept two-day weekends," she replied immediately.

Bethany's jaw dropped open, but he didn't figure the woman had really appreciated what his daughter could do when she set her mind to it.

Not until now.

"So in about five months, we'll drop a package in the

mail, addressed to Nikos at the University of Landing's English Department," Javier grinned.

"You're taking the credit for the machine translations," Suvi said sharply. "I am not legally a citizen of anywhere except *Altai*, and most places will not recognize that."

"I'll share it with you and Bethany," Javier countered. "I'm just another pretty face on this one. You two did the work."

It was Bethany's turn to blush. And shrug.

"It was your idea," she said, gesturing outward with both arms. "All of this. Your dream. The rest of us are really just along for the ride."

"Maybe," Javier replied. "In which case, I need to make sure we all get our money's worth out of it. Spending years or even months trying to fix that ship, unclutter the life support systems, and slowly bring it up while monitoring the roos for distress is time better spent off doing other things."

"Ride into town like one of those ancient cowboys from the vids?" Djamila chuckled. "Shoot the bad guys and ride off into the sunset?"

He turned a serious face towards her now.

"Yes," Javier replied.

She sobered, watching him. Nodded.

Javier turned to the others to bring them in on it. Bethany had earned her spot in this room because she understood the past. She and Suvi were every day making a better encyclopedia for him to consult when he needed to turn some obscure thought or long-long memory into a thing.

"The Rising Storm," he continued. "If we're lucky, *Kimmeria* turns into a thing that binds *Ormint* and *Trotau Skale* into a closer relationship from what little they have now. They'll need that if another war breaks out soon. And all of you know my thinking and logic on the topic. It's coming. I don't know when or where, but it will happen in my lifetime. *Kimmeria* did not present as a new, destabilizing technology that might have triggered it somehow, but that's retrospect. Only retrospect. Tomorrow, there will be something else we need to deal with."

"How much difference can we really make, Javier?" Bethany asked.

He turned to her now and let the smile wash all the grim seriousness off his bones. She blinked in surprise at his look.

"Go ask one of those tree-roos how much of a difference we just made in their lives," he said. "One of these days, the last generator would have failed. Or the life support systems would have collapsed. They would have all suffocated. Now, they get to go live in breeding zoos somewhere, if I had to guess. They'll make it into that future. That's why we're here. That's why we continue."

"To save the galaxy?" she pressed.

"You got anything better to do with your life, kid?"

ABOUT THE AUTHOR

Blaze Ward writes science fiction in the Alexandria Station universe (Jessica Keller, The Science Officer, The Story Road, etc.) as well as several other science fiction universes, such as Star Dragon, the Dominion, and more. He also writes odd bits of high fantasy with swords and orcs. In addition, he is the Editor and Publisher of *Boundary Shock Quarterly Magazine*. You can find out more at his website www.blazeward.com, as well as Facebook, Goodreads, and other places.

Blaze's works are available as ebooks, paper, and audio, and can be found at a variety of online vendors. His newsletter comes out regularly, and you can also follow his blog on his website. He really enjoys interacting with fans, and looks forward to any and all questions—even ones about his books!

Never miss a release!
If you'd like to be notified of new releases, sign up for my newsletter.

http://www.blazeward.com/newsletter/

Buy More!
Did you know that you can buy directly from my website?

https://www.blazeward.com/shop/

Connect with Blaze!

Web: www.blazeward.com
Boundary Shock Quarterly (BSQ):
https://www.boundaryshockquarterly.com/

ABOUT KNOTTED ROAD PRESS

Knotted Road Press fiction specializes in dynamic writing set in mysterious, exotic locations.

Knotted Road Press non–fiction publishes autobiographies, business books, cookbooks, and how–to books with unique voices.

Knotted Road Press creates DRM–free ebooks as well as high–quality print books for readers around the world.

With authors in a variety of genres including literary, poetry, mystery, fantasy, and science fiction, Knotted Road Press has something for everyone.

Knotted Road Press
www.KnottedRoadPress.com